Big Bad Bear

TERRY BOLRYDER

DEDICATION

For all my awesome bear fans!

CONTENTS

Acknowledgments   i

1   Chapter   Pg 1

2   Chapter   Pg 17

3   Chapter   Pg 27

4   Chapter   Pg 36

5   Chapter   Pg 51

6   Chapter   Pg 64

7   Chapter   Pg 77

8   Chapter   Pg 92

9   Chapter   Pg 103

10   Chapter   Pg 111

11   Chapter   Pg 124

12   Chapter   Pg 134

13   Chapter   Pg 146

14   Chapter   Pg 154

ACKNOWLEDGMENTS

Special thanks to all those who helped this book come to be.
You know who you are.

CHAPTER 1

Carly had to get out of this town.

She absentmindedly wiped down the tables at Lone Tree Bar and Grill once more. Anything to pass the time during the dead zone between lunch and dinner. The bar was deathly quiet in the afternoons, only frequented by the occasional jobless man looking to drown his sorrows or people who worked night shifts looking to take the edge off before work started.

The Lone Tree was one of several bars in Bearstone Village, a tiny town nestled at the base of a vast mountain range that held one of the world's most famous winter sports resorts, Bearstone Park. But unlike Bearstone Park, this town was old, rundown, and virtually empty during summers when the resorts were closed, since nobody would drive through a tiny place like this except to get to somewhere much nicer.

If only I could make enough to move out and get a fresh start someplace new, Carly thought to herself as she grabbed the rag she was using and tossed it into a small bucket.

She was grateful that Rob, the owner, had given her the job six months ago, since it was the only thing keeping her afloat right now. She was still several months behind on rent since the creditors were constantly haranguing her to make good on her other payments, but at least she was moving forward, not backward.

Around five or so, people would start milling in to grab a beer or a bite to eat, and things would pick up. Depending on tips, she could sometimes do all right, though most people in this town were just as poor as she was.

Carly had just started drying a few clean glasses when she was interrupted by the tinkle of the bells that hung over the front door. She looked up to see a huge shadow standing in the doorway. In walked a towering man wearing leather boots, roughed-up jeans, and a huge black leather jacket that bulged at the shoulders.

He probably stood at six feet six or so, a good foot or more taller than Carly. He had dark, unkempt hair that fell over his face in slight waves, which looked like a woman had just been running her hands through them, and steely blue eyes that watched her carefully, showing no emotion.

As he came into the light and nodded to Carly, she recognized his handsome, masculine face.

Zeus Wilson.

He walked over to his usual stool at the far corner of the bar. She could almost feel the ground rumble beneath her from the thump-thump of his huge boots as he moved, and despite his worn-looking clothes, she could make out incredibly muscled thighs straining his jeans and massive pecs and arms that looked ready to burst out of his jacket.

Zeus had come in a few times since Carly had worked here. After the first time, she'd asked Rob about him.

Apparently, he was a noted recluse who lived alone in the mountains and only came down occasionally to do business with locals.

"What can I get for you?" Carly asked from behind the bar where she stood. Even hunched over with his arms planted on the bar top, the man was humongous. His mere presence was intimidating.

"Whisky," Zeus answered in a husky tone that filled her with anticipation. He was so large, so masculine; it was impossible to not be aware of his presence.

"Which brand?" she asked, trying to keep the nervousness out of her voice.

"Any," he replied.

Carly grabbed a bottle of something mid-range and a shot glass. As she came over to where he was seated, she could feel his eyes following her every movement, intimidating but also thrilling. It made her scared to look directly at him for fear of making eye contact and seeing those striking blue irises, so she watched the ground as she came over.

She opened the bottle and moved to pour a shot for him when the bottle was gently whisked out of her hand. Carly looked up to see Zeus set the bottle beside him and pull something out of the pocket of his jacket with the other.

He slid money onto the bar in front of her. Her eyes widened as she looked down at it. A hundred was far too much, especially considering he was pouring his own drinks and making it less work for her.

"I can't take that," Carly said, pushing the bill toward him. The last thing she wanted to do was rip someone off. Especially someone like Zeus, who'd always been a good customer.

Zeus put his hand over hers, his huge fingers entirely enveloping it and the hundred. There was a slight roughness to his palm that she could feel on the top of her hand, and the light touch sent sparks of electricity through her fingers and down her spine, giving her goose bumps. He gently pushed her hand and the bill toward her, and she finally dared to look up and meet his piercing gaze.

His clear blue eyes were a deep royal blue. Intense, with a depth that seemed to go on forever.

Zeus said nothing, just shook his head slowly as he pressed her hand back along the smooth bar, the money underneath it. When his hand finally released hers, Carly let out the breath she hadn't realized she'd been holding.

The whole exchange could have lasted all of three seconds or several minutes. She wasn't sure. All she knew was the closer she got to him, the more he took her breath away.

Carly nodded in understanding, and for a moment, she thought she could see the smallest ghost of a smile at the corner of his mouth before he put the bottle to his lips and took a long swig. She couldn't help but admire at this distance his incredibly masculine features. His powerful, straight jaw. Thick brows that made his gaze even more intense. Tanned skin and broad cheekbones. And perfectly defined lips that pursed slightly as he drank.

It made her wonder what those lips would feel like on hers.

Carly's last relationship had gone down in flames only a year ago, leaving her stuck in this town, working off debts she'd likely never repay, and she wasn't eager to start something with a man again.

But something about Zeus made a woman want to try.

Her thoughts were interrupted by the clank of the bottle onto the counter, and Carly quickly went back to what she'd been doing before, hoping he hadn't noticed her gawking.

She went to the cash register to break the hundred into smaller amounts so she could put the excess into the tip jar. But when she opened the register, she saw it was out of twenties.

Rob kept all the cash in his office in a safe, and Carly knew they would need money in the register before the evening regulars came in anyway, so she exited the bar and headed for Rob's office.

"Excuse me for a moment," she said to Zeus, trying to sound formal but hearing something that sounded more like a squeak come out of her mouth.

The man didn't reply, just nodded, but still followed her intently with his eyes. As she walked past him, she could swear he was watching as she walked down the hallway that connected with the storage rooms and Rob's office. But when she turned around to look, all she saw was the huge man hunched over the bar and turned away from her.

She went through a door for employees only, turned down the hall, and came up to the thick wooden door that led into the office. Carly listened to see if he was playing his oldies rock station. She knew Rob didn't like to be interrupted if he was in the middle of doing financials or counting money, and the sure sign he was doing either of those was the sound of Lynyrd Skynyrd or Bob Seger coming from the office.

But instead of the sound of music, she heard voices coming from inside. Angry voices. She perked her ear closer to the door

"You're way behind on your payments, Rob. Where's the money you owe us?" said one voice, gruff and mean.

"I don't have it yet. I will by the end of the month." Rob sounded terrified.

"Do we have to remind you this is for your

protection, friend? If you can't make good on your part, then how are we supposed to keep you and your establishment safe from rival gangs in the area?" said another voice, this one more cool and conniving.

It sounded like extortion. She'd heard whispers from drunks and other locals about the town being under the control of a resident biker gang, the Red Devils, but she'd never seen any proof of it, and she wasn't one to pry into dangerous things.

She didn't know if she should run and call the police. If she did, it might be too late for them to do anything.

"Maybe we oughta teach him a lesson. Give him a taste of what'll happen if he doesn't meet the deadline by the end of the month," said the first voice.

Carly couldn't wait any longer. She had to do something. She turned to go to the bar and use the phone. But she'd only taken one step when the floor gave a loud creak beneath her.

Carly cursed and froze, hoping the men inside hadn't heard the wood betray her.

"Did you hear that?"

"Go outside and check it out. I'll stay here."

Carly knew they'd found her out, so she rushed for the end of the hall and the door that led back into the main restaurant area. Behind her, she heard the door fly open with a bang, followed by loud footsteps coming up on her fast. Though the hallway wasn't that long, it felt like a mile. Her heart was pounding as she ran.

Angry voices muttered behind her, and she knew they were close. She sprinted for the door and pushed it open, but before she could make it out, a hand grabbed the back of her shirt and yanked her back into the poorly lit hall.

She was shoved against the wall and realized she was surrounded by three terrifying men dressed in various combinations of grubby-looking biker gear. One had a headband that was red and black. Another wore dark sunglasses. And the last had a smug grin that showed missing teeth.

"What do we have here?" he snarled.

"Rob didn't tell us he had such a hot piece of ass working for him," said another as he leered.

She was totally caged in by the three of them. At the other end of the hall, she could still hear someone else inside Rob's office, making threats, but she was too frightened to make out any of it.

"What did you hear?" asked the one in front of her. He was by far the meanest-looking of the three.

"N-nothing," Carly stuttered.

"Really?" he asked doubtfully.

"Honest, I swear. I don't know anything." Carly tried to sound convincing, tried to keep herself together. But she'd never been more scared in her life, and she could feel tears starting to form at the corners of her eyes.

Everything had just gone wrong for her, ever since she came to this town. No, even before that, if she really thought about it.

"Maybe we can take her as a down payment on Rob's debt. I don't think he would mind," the one with missing teeth said with an evil grin. He leaned in, and she cringed away, avoiding his fetid breath as he tried to kiss her.

In that very second, the door behind them that led into the bar whooshed open with incredible speed. A huge figure stood on the threshold, looming just a few feet away.

All three men turned around at the same time and looked up at Zeus, standing at his full, intimidating height, hands clenched and blue eyes glaring down at them.

She could feel the rage emanating from him, and somehow it made her feel secure, like everything was going to be all right.

"Let the woman go," Zeus growled, assessing the

men before him like a predator eyeing prey.

"Who the hell are you?" the mean-looking one spat, stepping forward. All three of the thugs were large, burly men. But they were tiny hills compared to the mountain that was Zeus.

"None of your business. Just let the lady go and there won't be any trouble," Zeus said darkly, taking a small step forward.

The man on the right stepped forward. "How about you go fu—"

His curse was interrupted by a loud crack as Zeus's fist connected straight with the man's jaw, sending him flying into the wall to Carly's right with a loud thump.

For a split second, the other two turned and looked at their comrade, stunned. Then, in unison, both men charged at Zeus. He grabbed them both easily and pulled them into the main eating area, away from Carly.

Carly saw the man motionless to her side, but she still heard an angry voice coming from the direction of Rob's office, so she took the opening and came out of the hallway, ducking behind a table in the corner of the restaurant and hoping to stay out of sight.

Zeus held both men by the collar, then tossed

one to the side while the other swung wildly at him.
He kicked that one in the gut, and the man flew
backward, crashing through chairs and tables. The
other man lunged at Zeus, who whirled around to
meet him with a solid punch to the nose that sent the
thug reeling back into a table and then falling to the
ground, out cold.

Despite his sheer size, Zeus moved with
incredible precision and speed. Most men around
these parts were no strangers to bar fights, but the
way Zeus fought was more practiced and honed. The
kind of skill that came from a lifetime of training.

In that moment, another man came in, swearing
up a storm and running at Zeus. It was the one who
had stayed in Rob's office, and Carly guessed he was
probably the highest in command of the group,
based on his size and how he'd been the one giving
commands earlier.

"You picked the wrong people to mess with,
stranger," he said.

Zeus said nothing. Just replied by grabbing the
charging man by his collar and throwing him over his
shoulder like a sack of potatoes. The man shrieked as
he landed square in the middle of a large table, which
buckled beneath him and crashed onto the ground in
a cloud of splinters.

The man groaned as he rolled over and tried to get up. Zeus didn't let up, just walked over to the man, examined him for a split second, and gave him one swift blow to the head, knocking him out.

For a moment, the room was still, not a sound disrupting the odd quiet as Zeus looked around one last time, then came over to the table Carly was hidden behind.

Her blood froze. Not only was this the largest, most badass man she had ever seen in her entire life. But he was also dangerous. What would he do with her?

Zeus knelt in front of her and reached out his hand. The anger and coldness were gone from his eyes. Instead, there was a gentle warmth that eased her worry.

"You're not safe here. You need to come with me," he said, his voice low.

Carly's mind willed her to move, but her body was still shaking from the adrenaline of the past couple minutes. Everything had happened so fast.

"But, my job… My shift doesn't—"

"There's no time for that now," he said, cutting her off.

Carly looked around and saw the motionless bodies of the men around her. If they really were from the Red Devils, then Zeus was right; she wasn't safe here. But maybe they weren't. Maybe they were just loan sharks Rob had gotten in too deep with.

Zeus looked impatiently at her, then swooped her up into his arms. "Here, let me help you," he said, more commanding than asking.

The feeling of being picked up off the ground and held in the humongous man's arms was surreal. Carly was by no means a slight woman, so she'd never understood what it felt like to be carried. But as Zeus turned and made for the door, opening it with his foot and walking across the small parking lot, she instantly began to feel much better, much safer.

Even if Zeus was a complete stranger and a total mystery to her, there was something about him that felt right. She was safe with him. Somehow she just knew it.

He walked toward what Carly assumed must be his motorcycle, a big, black Harley with shining chrome and a pristine paint job. She had no clue how much bikes like this cost, but she assumed it was probably pretty expensive. Which made no sense from the stories she'd heard about him being half civilized and living in the mountains all alone.

Zeus set Carly down on the rear part of the large

leather seat, quite gracefully to her surprise, and then handed her a huge helmet.

"Put this on," he said.

She didn't ask questions, just put on the helmet that was clearly for a head much larger than hers and buckled the strap tightly so it wouldn't come off. Zeus climbed onto the bike, and she felt the shocks lurch under his sheer size as he clicked the stand into its place and started the engine with his foot. The motorcycle roared to life as he took a pair of large sunglasses out of his coat pocket and put them on.

From behind Zeus, she could see just how broad-shouldered he was and just how big his muscles really were. Part of Carly longed to slip her hands under his jacket and see just what he felt like, but the more rational part of her still told her she was crazy for just leaving with him like this when she barely knew him.

As her mind was still racing, Zeus turned back to her, his mirrored sunglasses showing her reflection.

"You'll want to hold on," he said. Then he put the engine into gear. They moved forward, and Carly felt her body sway backward, causing her to wrap her arms tightly around Zeus in panic. She'd never been on a motorcycle before, let alone ridden behind someone, so the feeling was entirely new to her.

Zeus drove out of the parking lot and down the

main thoroughfare that comprised most of downtown Bearstone Village. He turned the motorcycle onto a small side rode that pointed straight toward the hills and mountains that rose into the towering range where Bearstone Park was located.

But instead of heading toward Bearstone Park, this road went in a different direction. They drove up steep paved roads that winded along hillsides and passed through endless acres of ageless pine trees.

I must be crazy. This guy really does live out in the middle of nowhere, she thought. They turned off onto side road after side road, as if navigating a maze where only Zeus knew the layout. Carly held on tight as the Harley roared through the silent forests, and she couldn't help but relish the feel of his tight muscles under the smooth leather of his jacket, despite the stress of the situation and the knowledge that she'd only barely escaped something terrible.

But she trusted Zeus. He'd helped her when no one else had, and for that, she'd give him a chance.

CHAPTER 2

Zeus had no clue what he was going to do next. For someone whose entire livelihood and survival in the past had rested on carefully made plans and executing them perfectly, this was certainly not something he could have anticipated.

His mate was here with him, riding on his motorcycle, driving toward his house in the mountains.

At least, that's what his bear had called her when he'd first laid eyes on her several months ago.

Zeus hated going into town, preferring the solitude of the mountains where his bear could roam free and he could enjoy the quiet of the forest. After so many years of fighting and war, he was happy to have a place of his own where he could spend his days in peace.

But every now and then, the urge to go somewhere where other humans gathered hit him. Which was exactly where he'd found Carly. From the instant he saw her, he knew. His bear called out to him, telling him she was the one for him. And for bear shifters, when you knew, you just knew.

It didn't hurt that her luscious body had perfect curves, just the way he liked. A gorgeous, round ass. Huge breasts and wide hips. A delicate, heart-shaped face. A sparkling personality, despite her shyness. Nice brown hair the color of bear fur and light-brown eyes the color of whisky that looked amazing with her deep skin tone. And lush red lips he wished he could kiss.

She was everything he'd ever dreamed of. Everything he'd never thought possible after getting out of the military. After all, women wanted someone polite and social, not someone who'd made a living with battle skills and now lived as a recluse and occasionally turned into a bear.

Yet he hadn't been able to stay away. Her warm smile, the way she looked at him welcomingly when he came in, it all kept calling to him, drawing him down from the mountain to see her again.

But he hadn't been able to figure out a way to

initiate something with her. Whenever he was around her, he got tongue-tied. He could command a battalion of troops, interrogate the most sinister men the world had to offer, and survive for weeks in the most unforgiving climates on nothing but raw discipline and his survival skills. But for some reason, the idea of talking to Carly made his heart race more than being under enemy fire ever had.

Of course, Zeus's friend and former squad mate Ares found the irony of the situation hilarious to no end. Zeus, however, did not.

He turned onto the last road that lead up to his cabin, and he could feel Carly hold on tightly as the motorcycle leaned and hugged the edge of the road on their way up the mountain. He loved the feel of her body pressed against his, her arms holding on to him as she trusted him to take her to safety.

The incident back at the bar with the gangsters had been fortuitous for Zeus, if unfortunate for everyone else involved. Compared to the various insurgents, trained mercenaries, and cartel gangsters he'd fought over the years, those thugs had been child's play. But the whole thing still bothered him. The Red Devils's influence over the town was supposed to be waning, not growing stronger. He and Ares had been keeping an eye on it ever since they'd moved back here after getting out of the military.

He made a mental note to talk about it with Ares tomorrow. Right now, he just wanted to make sure Carly was safe.

They finally reached the two-story cabin where Zeus lived, and he pulled out his phone, pressing the necessary buttons and inputting the proper code to disable the alarm perimeter surrounding his house before he drove up and parked. If anything bigger than a badger came within a hundred feet of his place, Zeus wanted to know.

He drove up to the house, killed the engine, and kicked the stand for the bike, then came off.

Time to see what his mate thought of his home.

* * *

Carly couldn't believe her eyes. The place was like something out of a dream. Or an issue of Mountain Living magazine, if such a thing existed.

The house was a two-story cabin, though it looked much bigger and more spacious than one would typically describe as being a cabin. It had a wide, covered porch and a tall, vaulted roof that rose high into the center of the clearing where the house was built. All around in every direction, Carly could see pine and aspen forest going on forever, up and down the hillside.

She wasn't sure just how long they'd been driving. But she guessed it was easily long enough to be far away from Bearstone Village, or any other people at all for that matter.

Carly stood up and came off the bike, feeling wobbly after the new experience of riding on a motorcycle. She took off the helmet and handed it to Zeus, who took it and walked up the steps, motioning for her to follow.

She couldn't help but notice just how quiet it was up here. If it were any other man, she'd be scared for her life. But Zeus had already proven to her that he wasn't going to hurt her. And even aside from that, there was something else about him that drew her in. Something that eased her normal cautionary responses and made her feel safe somehow.

When she came inside, she noticed how organized and nice the place looked. A little spartan as far as actual decorations or color, but there was lots of furniture and everything looked modern and new. Cabinets, tables, couches, everything looked as if it had been hand-carved and uniquely made just for this place.

The men Carly had dated in the past had pretty much been slobs, so she was surprised to see that Zeus seemed to take a lot of pride in his surroundings.

"Did you do this?" Carly asked, running her hand over the soft lacquer of a hand-carved hall tree at the entrance to the house.

"Some of it. Most of it is done by a friend of mine who makes furniture. You might meet him in the next day or two," he said, taking off his huge leather jacket and hanging it on the hall tree.

Carly almost gulped at the sight before her. Under his jacket, Zeus was even bigger than she'd thought. He wore a tight gray T-shirt that did little to hide the rippling muscles underneath the thin fabric. She could make out every perfectly defined muscle across his chest and arms. A body honed through years of practice.

His broad shoulders connected strong, heavily muscled arms. His squared pecs led to defined, bulging abs. Even his forearms were corded with tight muscle, tapering down to beautiful, large male hands. The kind you just wanted on you.

And now that she was standing right next to him, she realized fully just how small she was next to him. The top of her head probably only barely reached the middle of his chest, and in every direction she looked in front of her, he was there, filling her vision.

Zeus looked down at her with those intense blue eyes, and she had no idea what he was thinking at this moment.

Part of her wanted to run. The other part wanted to pull him down for a kiss and maybe more.

For now, though, she had to stay focused. She reminded herself just how poorly her last relationship had gone, and that cooled her quickly heating body temperature enough for her to think a little more clearly about the problems at hand.

Like what was going to happen next, now that she was alone in a mountain cabin with a man she barely knew.

"Here, I'll show you to your bedroom," he said, heading up a stairway to their right. She followed, still not sure what to make of the whole situation. They went down a short hallway that ended with a large room, which she assumed was the guest bedroom.

"You can sleep here," he said. The room was surprisingly comfortable-looking, with a big queen-size bed and a full set of the same type of hand-carved furniture she'd seen in the living room. Much nicer than the dumpy apartment she'd been calling home the past year.

"I… I appreciate what you did for me back in the bar, but I can't just stay here," she said. "I mean, I have a job back home, and I have an apartment I'm renting, and… I barely know you."

He tilted his head to the side, and a lock of dark hair fell over his forehead. His hair was loose and thick and waved around his face and brushed over his collar. He stared at her for a moment, his strong arms crossed over his chest as his eyes narrowed in thought.

"Um, did I say something wrong?" she asked quietly.

Zeus shook his head. "But I can't let you leave."

"So I'm just supposed to stay here? Overnight, with you?"

Zeus nodded.

It was crazy. How could he just bring a random stranger into his home?

"Will I be going back home tomorrow?" she asked.

He shook his head and lowered his brows.

"Why not?"

"Not safe," he said solemnly.

"What about my stuff? I can't just sleep over with what I'm wearing." The black button-up and jeans she wore for work were thankfully fairly comfortable, but not that comfortable.

"I'll call a friend. He'll get your stuff," he said.

Carly didn't know what to make of his stiff, almost stern demeanor. But as he avoided her gaze, she almost thought maybe he was nervous. But that'd be ridiculous. How could such a tall, menacing, obviously capable man be intimidated by her? He'd dispatched the men in the bar like they were yesterday's garbage.

She folded her arms and thought things over. He was probably right that it wasn't safe to go home. Awkward as the situation was, she was probably safest here.

"How will your friend get inside my place?" Carly asked. She knew the building's outer door was usually left ajar anyway, and her apartment only had one half-functional lock, but she wasn't going to admit that.

"Not a problem," he replied nonchalantly.

Carly wasn't going to ask what that meant. If the people Zeus associated with were anything like him, they probably had a lot of hidden talents too.

She was definitely grateful for what Zeus had done for her back at the bar. And she was grateful he was so willing to bring her to his own place and watch out for her. Already, he was nothing like any man she'd ever met. But her heart warned her to be careful. She tended to get her hopes up too easily. Tended to fall into things with men who never turned out as good as she thought they were.

"You relax. I'll make dinner," Zeus said, turning to leave suddenly. "If you need anything, let me know."

Part of her groaned in disappointment at the sight of his broad shoulders retreating down the hall. But then she realized how hungry she was. Carly thought back to earlier in the day and remembered she'd skipped lunch because there had been an influx of diners around noon. And after that, she'd just forgotten about it.

Whatever was going to happen, she could wait until after dinner to figure it out. Right now, the cool air and her swiftly relaxing body was leaving her exhausted from the day's exertion and stress. And the only thing that sounded better than dinner was a quick nap.

She lay down and instantly fell asleep.

CHAPTER 3

Zeus listened quietly at the door of the guest bedroom. With his bear senses, he could pick up even the slightest motion or the quietest noises with his hearing. Inside, his mate rustled lightly and gave a little snore as she napped.

His mate. Sooner or later, she was going to have to hear that from his own mouth. But for now, it was enough just to have her so near.

As much as he wanted to let her sleep, dinner was fast getting cold, and he was certain she would be hungry. He'd sensed the tension in her before she'd turned in. And Zeus wasn't going to stand for his mate ever going hungry. Not on his watch.

Zeus tapped the door lightly a few times, hoping it wouldn't startle Carly. There was the sound of sheets shifting, and for a split second, he imagined being there with her, on top of her, making her scream his name in pleasure.

He shook his head, hoping to clear the thought from his mind. Never had he been this dumbfounded by a woman. Never before had anyone had this sort of effect on him. Then again, she was his mate. She would always mean more to him than anyone else ever could. All he could do was treat her right and hope the feelings he had for her would become mutual.

Carly came up to the door and opened it, looking a little drowsy, her hair sticking out of its ponytail in several places. It looked so soft, as always, and he had to restrain himself from wanting to touch it.

"I made some dinner, if you're hungry," Zeus said.

Carly took in a long whiff and smiled. "Smells delicious. Are you sure it's okay? I'm not imposing or anything?"

"It's fine," he said, letting her walk past him and down the stairs toward the kitchen.

For dinner, Zeus had cooked up some steaks and potatoes. He certainly hadn't learned to be a master chef in the service, but nothing made the men happier than a good cookout with delicious grilled meat, so Zeus knew enough to get by.

He watched as Carly's eyes lit up at the dinner laid out on the table. Outside, the sun had already set, and the warm evening light was turning a cool blue that settled over the surrounding forest around them. His favorite time of day.

He pulled the chair up for her to sit down, then took a seat himself. He quickly served up a large portion for Carly, which she responded to with a suspicious eyebrow.

"This isn't a trick or some sicko game for you, is it? Rescuing women and bringing them back here to feed them ridiculous amounts of food?"

"No," Zeus said, a small smile teasing the corners of his lips. "It's not every day a woman like you needs rescuing. And as for dinner, I just know you're hungry."

"How did you...? Never mind," she said, turning to the food in front of her and cutting several bites before trying it. She took one bite and chewed slowly. Zeus waited eagerly for her reaction.

"Aw hell," she said, looking both pleased and peeved at the same time.

"Is something wrong?"

"No. That's the problem. It's delicious. I've never tasted something this good before."

"How is that a problem?" Zeus asked, confused.

"I was hoping it would be as bad as all the other cooking men have tried to do for me so I could stop seeing you as Mr. Perfect," she said, waving a fork at him before taking several more bites at one time and eating rapidly.

"Would you like me to stop?" he asked.

"No, don't. It's nice to have a guy like you around. Someone who actually gives a crap about things like owning his own place or being able to cook," she said.

"What do you mean?" Zeus asked, leaning back in his chair and listening intently.

Carly looked at him questioningly for a moment, as if not believing he actually wanted to hear more. But when he didn't interrupt her, she finished another bite and continued.

"Let's just say I haven't had the best luck with relationships in the past. At best, they expect everything from you and do nothing to show they actually care. At worst, they straight up abandon you and leave you to the wolves. The last man I took up with falls under that category," she said, cutting her steak vigorously, as if the memory of it put her on edge.

"You don't have to talk about it," Zeus said, not

wanting to open up old wounds.

"No, it's fine. It's what brought me out here actually," she said, taking another bite between sentences and closing her eyes as she moaned a little from the flavor. It made Zeus think of making her moan in another way. "This last guy, we were together for a couple years. He never made any commitments, but I figured being a girl with average looks like mine and the kind of bad family history I come from, it was the best I was going to do."

"You're gorgeous," Zeus interjected. It made him angry to think of anyone that could have ever called her average or less than. To him, she was stunning.

Carly looked up at him, and he saw a faint flush spread over her cheeks just before she stifled a smile and continued her story. "So anyway, a year ago, he gets this genius idea to come back to his hometown and open a business. A coffee shop to be exact. And I figure, why not? By that point in my life, I was broke from having to bail my brother out of prison and trying to pay off my mom's rent because her drinking meant she couldn't hold a job. But I was done living my life for them, letting them keep me from ever moving forward. A new place, a change of scenery, a chance at getting paid more than minimum wage for once in my life? It sounded like it was worth a shot."

Zeus felt anger burn through him at what his mate had been through, but he was glad she'd found her way here. Still, he was disgusted by her family.

In his case, he had no family. His mom had left early and his dad had been mostly absent, not caring when Zeus left at eighteen to enroll in the military. But no family was probably better than the kind of family Carly had.

She sighed and moved her food around on her plate, drawing his attention back to her. "So we moved here, opened up shop, and what do you know, but my boyfriend goes on a spending spree? The second the bank gave us a business card, he spent it on everything from a new TV to fancy shoes, all the while talking about how much money the business was going to bring in and how we were going to be rich," Carly said, speaking animatedly with her hands, then taking another bite of steak.

Zeus could tell from the second he heard the story that her ex was a complete tool, not even worthy of being called a man. In his mind, it was a male's duty to love and protect and provide for their mate, no matter the circumstances.

"So what happened?" Zeus asked.

"As expected, things tanked fast. The business

didn't do too bad, especially the baked goods. But between my ex's spending, him missing work all the time, and the incredible loan debt we had taken on, it was only a matter of months before the business went bottoms up and we had to shut down. And being the idiot I was, I had cosigned personally on all the loans. So when my ex skipped town one day with a passing trucker, it all fell on me to pay back," she said with an annoyed sigh.

"Did you ever think of leaving too?" Zeus asked.

"All my family ever did was run from problems. But I decided to stay and fight, even if it was going to take me the rest of my life to finally break free," she responded, finishing off the last bite of steak.

That made Zeus happy. Not the fact that she'd been through so much crap in her life, but that she was such a strong woman. Someone who didn't run when things got tough.

"So here I am. Working as a waitress at the town bar." She paused for a moment, looking vulnerable for the first time this evening. "You probably think I'm dumb as dirt for doing all of that though, don't you? Getting in over my head, getting stuck out here in the middle of nowhere with more debt than the government hanging over me?"

Zeus reached out a hand to cover one of hers

across the table. He could see sadness in her eyes, and he wanted to make it all go away if he could. But even if not, he wanted her to know he would never judge her.

And if she allowed it, he would be hers forever.

"No, I don't think you did anything wrong. You took a chance, and the people you trusted most were the ones who failed, not you. I think you're an incredibly strong woman, Carly. Maybe fate brought you out here for a reason," Zeus said.

Carly didn't recoil at his touch, but instead, just smiled a little. Her hand was soft and warm beneath his, and just the slightest feel of her skin made him come alive inside, made his bear roar with approval.

"Well, if I'm honest, Bearstone Village isn't all that bad," she said, her eyes roving over Zeus's chest unabashedly before looking back up to him. His mate liked his body. That was definitely good.

"I'm glad you think so," he said warmly.

Right then, Zeus's phone gave several loud beeps, and he quickly pulled it out to see what the source of the interruption was.

"What is it?" Carly asked.

"It's the perimeter. Someone's outside," Zeus said, flipping to the camera that had a view of the front porch.

"Perimeter? What do you mean?" Carly asked, sounding worried.

"I have a field of sensors that let me know if anyone is within fifty feet of the house. I don't like unexpected company."

"What do you mean unexpected?"

A second later, a loud knock sounded on the door.

CHAPTER 4

Carly was petrified.

Just a second ago, she'd been enjoying the feel of Zeus's hand over hers and the buzzing warmth it caused to build in her. But now there was someone unknown at the door, and she was suddenly and painfully aware of the fact that she was in a house in an unknown location with a stranger, and the same men that had threatened her earlier in the day could be outside right now.

"There's nothing to worry about. I'll go get it," Zeus said, standing and leaving the kitchen for the front door, out of her sight. The moment he was gone, she wished him back. Even if he was a stranger, he was a stranger she felt safe with.

Carly heard the door open and two low male

voices speaking. One was Zeus's. The other was a voice she'd never heard before, still low and masculine but more amicable, friendlier sounding. The sound stopped, followed by two pairs of big feet coming down the hall toward the kitchen.

Around the corner appeared Zeus again, followed by another man who was almost equally huge and every bit as hot.

Carly couldn't help but stare agape at the two men before her. Ares was around the same height as Zeus but with tanned skin and boyish features and golden-blond hair with the slightest hint of a curl to it.

"Carly, I'd like you to meet my friend, Ares. Ares, this is Carly," Zeus introduced.

"Ares? As in the god of war?" Carly asked, befuddled.

"One and the same. Charmed," the man said with a smile, offering a hand, which Carly took. His hand was much rougher and worn, and guessing from the dusty denim and heavy leather boots he wore, he did something in construction. His deep-green eyes looked amused as they shook hands.

"He's the one I called to go get your things while you were asleep," Zeus said.

"Yeah. I also fixed your lock while I was at it.

That thing was so old and busted. I only had to jiggle it a few times for it to open. The new one should work a lot better," he said, handing over a duffel bag and putting it next to Carly's seat. "Your stuff."

"T-thanks," she stuttered, looking down at the duffel and then back at the two men. Ares had the same rough, handsome looks as Zeus but with a calmer, friendlier demeanor. Still, she preferred Zeus's dark, silent strength.

Ares grinned slightly and leaned into Zeus. "I think she likes you," he whispered to his friend a little too loudly.

"I'm right here, you know," Carly said.

"Hey, who can blame you? Our man Zeus here is built like a Greek god," Ares said playfully, poking at Zeus, who didn't appear to be amused at all by the antics.

"So Zeus and Ares, that can't be your real names," she said.

"Well, no. They're our call signs from the military. Except for Zeus here, who was unfortunate enough to have that for his birth name. But it just sort of fit him, and those of us in his squad picked names to match."

She eyed him skeptically. "You seem too friendly to be the god of war," she said doubtfully.

Ares grinned. "You should see me with a rocket launcher."

That made her laugh, and she turned to Zeus curiously. "So you were in the army? Like, special forces or something like that?"

"Something like that," Zeus said cryptically, not seeming eager to talk about it. "I can't really tell you more than that."

"Top secret," Ares said, putting a finger up to his lips playfully.

"So are there any other Greek gods around here I should know about?" Carly asked, looking between them.

"Just Hades. And he's too busy ruling the underworld to be bothered these days," Ares answered.

"Literally or figuratively?" Carly asked.

"You'll know if you ever meet him," Zeus said, then turned to Ares. "We need to talk about the Devils."

"I know," Ares said, sitting on a chair in the kitchen and spreading his long legs over another. "I heard about what happened down at the bar. I thought we weren't getting involved with the Devils just yet."

Zeus joined him at the table, and Carly sat next to

him, feeling safest at his side. Ares seemed like a nice enough person, but she knew Zeus better.

"They were extorting the owner, and Carly accidentally got involved. I had to intervene," he said, and she could hear the low growl of withheld anger in his voice.

Ares's green eyes flicked to her. "Ah, of course." The corners of his mouth lifted in a slight grin. "So, Carly, are you by any chance single?" he asked out of the blue.

Carly's mouth opened in shock, and from the corner of her eyes, she saw Zeus's expression tighten. She looked over to see a small vein twitch at the corner of his brow as he frowned at his friend.

"I don't see how that's any of your business," Zeus said tersely.

She looked between them, not really understanding what was going on. Was he being possessive of her? That wouldn't make sense.

"Hey, it's just a question," Ares replied, raising his hands in mock defense. "Carly's a gorgeous girl, and there aren't a lot of ladies out here." He sent Zeus a teasing glance. "Can't fault a man for trying."

"I'm not taken," she said quietly. "But I'm not really looking either."

"You don't have to answer him," Zeus said

irritably. "And anyway, we're supposed to be talking about the Devils. Carly, if you want to turn in for the night, you're welcome to. Or you can stay and listen."

"I'm good for a while," Carly said. "I don't like to sleep right after eating, and if there's anything important that needs to be discussed, then I want to be here for it."

Plus, she was kind of enjoying watching Zeus interact with Ares. He brought out a side of Zeus she hadn't seen, one she liked.

Zeus raised an eyebrow at her but didn't question her further. Instead, he turned to Ares. "All right. So what do they know in town about what happened today, and how did you hear about it?"

"I heard it from some of my construction guys that happened to be working across the street. You made quite a commotion. Not enough to draw the whole town, obviously, but enough to let people know. I think all anyone knows is a bar fight broke out, but everyone was gone before people started coming in for the evening."

"So nobody else knows about the Devils's involvement?"

"Except for the Red Devils at the bar and probably the owner, Rob, yeah. Pretty lucky, in my opinion."

"Lucky and unlucky. If there had been other people that had called the cops, they wouldn't have done anything about it anyway. They're too scared of the Devils to mess with them. If we want to stop them, it'll be up to us."

"What do the Red Devils have to do with all of this?" Carly asked.

Zeus looked over at her, a long, discerning glance that seemed to be appraising just how much he wanted to say. After a prolonged moment, he spoke.

"About a decade or so ago, they were a small biker gang that was displaced by a bigger rival gang out somewhere in the Midwest. For some reason, when they rolled into this town, they set up camp here and haven't left since. Though they're no big-time operation, they still practically run the town from the background," Zeus said.

"Extortion, money laundering, arms trading, drugs. The usual," Ares added. "A little place like Bearstone Village is a great spot to be if you don't want anyone finding you. They've been messing with the town businesses without anyone doing anything about it for years. But ever since Zeus and I have been here, we've been keeping an eye on it."

Carly wondered if that was why Zeus had come to the bar so much. But it didn't make sense, because she'd never seen trouble there before today.

"What about the police or even the FBI?" Carly asked.

"Like I mentioned, the police are afraid. And the regional FBI office has no proof that would make it care about a little nowhere town like Bearstone Village. And the people here are too scared to complain," Ares said.

"That's not to say we're not fighting the good fight. Zeus and I have been studying them and waiting for the right moment. But it's slow going, and the last thing we want to do is turn my hometown into a war zone."

"Well, that still might happen sooner than we thought," Zeus said to Ares.

"So how do I play into all of this?" Carly asked.

"You just happened to be in the wrong place at the wrong time. They would have silenced you, or worse, if I hadn't been there. But as it is, they aren't going to sit back and let you be. You're a witness, and they're going to want you out of the way."

She gulped. "So now what do I do?"

Ares grinned and walked over to Zeus, putting an arm around him as the other man stayed straight faced. "Just stay here with my man Zeus. If he can't keep you safe, no one can."

She frowned. "Still, it's not your problem, and I hate to be a bother—"

"You're not a bother," Zeus said. "I'm happy to have you here."

"And this guy spends way too much time alone," Ares said, teasing. "You'll be doing him a favor, staying with him for a few days in his lonely mountain cabin."

"You'll be safe with me, Carly." Zeus looked her straight in the eyes, causing something thrilling to zoom through her, straight down to her toes. "I promise."

"And you can bet he means it. This guy always makes good on his promises. There was this one time back in the service where he—"

"Not now, Ares," Zeus said sternly, cutting him off.

Carly laughed and then let out a long, relieved breath. "All right. You've convinced me." She gave Zeus a small smile. "I'd be grateful if you let me stay with you."

Zeus nodded at her. It was settled. "Ares and our colleague Hades will keep eyes and ears out down in town to see if the Devils are planning on making any moves. I'll stay here with you and guard you twenty-four-seven."

"Wait, what about my job?" Carly asked. If she didn't go back to the bar, she couldn't pay bills. If she missed payments, the debt would increase.

"Don't worry about it," Zeus said. "I'll have Ares check into your accounts in town and make sure they get paid regularly."

"I can't just let you pay my bills," she said, eyes widening in shock.

"Let him," Ares said. "The man's a whiz at investments. He's saved half the businesses in town when the crooked bank wouldn't help them."

Zeus shook his head as if the praise embarrassed him and he wanted it to stop. "All that matters right now is your safety, Carly," he said. "But if things do settle down and your job isn't available, Ares and I own several businesses in town, so finding a job for you won't be a problem at all."

"I'd definitely hire you," Ares said with a wicked wink.

Zeus frowned. "On second thought, we'll find a job for you somewhere other than his construction company." He glared, unamused, at Ares. His expression gentled as he turned back to Carly. "But we'll make sure and make it right after this is over. After all, if we'd dealt with the Devils sooner, maybe you'd never have gotten involved."

"It's not your fault," she said. "I'm just glad you were there at the right time." She met his gaze shyly, and he stared back, a warm, intent expression in his deep-blue gaze. Though he had a hard, masculine face, whenever he looked at her, he seemed to soften.

Maybe she was just letting herself get carried away, but she felt somehow special to him. She looked away as heat began to rise in her at the thought of them being alone together in the cabin for more than a few days.

Just his presence turned her on. She didn't know how she was going to make it.

As if sensing something suddenly, Ares stood and made to leave. "Well, looks like you don't need me anymore right now. You two take care," he said, nodding to his friend, then tipping an imaginary hat to Carly before walking out. "And don't worry about the sensors. I won't forget to take care of them on my way out this time," he said before the door opened, then closed.

As soon as the door was shut and the sound of Ares's boots walking down the front steps faded, Carly was acutely aware of just how quiet the cabin was and just how close Zeus was sitting right next to her, his body so much larger compared to hers.

Carly squirmed in her chair, unsure what to do

next. She was in a new house, depending on a man she barely knew and was extremely attracted to. It made her feel awkward.

Zeus seemed to sense this, and he stood up, grabbing her duffel bag from the ground. "Do you want to sleep now?" he asked.

Carly tried to stifle a yawn that came out of nowhere. Then she nodded her head yes and stood to follow Zeus upstairs.

Aside from a few lights in the living room, the rest of the house was dark, and through the windows, Carly could see the house was surrounded by pervasive blackness on all sides, illuminated by only the slightest hint of moonlight.

But despite the darkness, she felt safe here with Zeus. It was an odd feeling, one she'd never really had with another man before in her life.

He turned on a light and led her down the hall, and she folded her arms around herself, trying to ignore the growing chemistry between them. It was hard not to start falling for the man, with the way he was already taking better care of her than anyone had in her life.

Not to mention the fact that she'd always been attracted to him.

His back spanned almost the entire hallway as

they walked toward the room at the end. She felt when she was with him, nothing in the world could hurt her. But what would happen when it was all over? She needed to be careful not to get ideas too quickly or she'd just be hurt when it all ended.

"Are you sure you really want to do all of this for me?" Carly felt compelled to ask.

"Of course. Why wouldn't I?" he asked solemnly.

Carly looked up at him, and in the dim light of the hallway, she could see his bright, blue eyes watching her closely. They were the color of a clear mountain lake, cool and inviting and intense all at the same time.

She tightened her arms around her self-consciously. "I don't know. Because you barely know me. Because no one ever does things like this for me. I'm not the kind of girl men sweep off her feet. I'm just… average."

Zeus folded his arms and gave her a piercing gaze that seemed to see straight into her soul, as if they were the only two people on the face of the planet right now and she was the only one that mattered to him.

She wasn't imagining it. There was something between them, and it wasn't just on her end. Carly gulped slightly and couldn't help but enjoy the way his muscles bulged in his arms and shoulders with his arms crossed like that. The way it accentuated his pecs as well.

"There's a lot more to you than you're giving yourself credit for. And as for being average…" He paused as his eyes roved up and down her body. "I've never met a more beautiful woman in my entire life. Ever," he said, his voice low and husky. Just the sound rattled her to her core and made her wet. Made her want more with him. Right here, right now.

She'd give anything for just one kiss.

Zeus didn't move for a long moment that could have lasted forever. She wanted to devour him with her eyes, and if she wasn't entirely wrong about him, he wanted to do the same.

"Carly, I…" Zeus began, sounding hesitant as he stepped forward, closer to her.

"Yes?" she said breathlessly. His lips, so gorgeous. Just one kiss.

He stopped right in front of her, just a breath away. If he just leaned down a little and she got up on her toes—

Then he took a deep breath and pulled away. "I hope you sleep well. Let me know if you need anything," he said, breaking eye contact and walking past her across the hall. "Good night," he said, sending her one last glance before going into his room and closing the door behind him.

Carly felt like someone had waved a brownie under her nose and then walked away with it. She opened the door to her room, went in, and closed it behind her before plopping onto the bed with a frustrated sigh.

CHAPTER 5

The next day, Carly just wanted to stay in bed.
She was still embarrassed from that awkward
moment last night with Zeus outside her bedroom
door.

She could hear him moving about the cabin, hear
the sizzle of something in the kitchen, smell delicious
breakfast smells. Any moment, he would show up
and she'd have to act like nothing was bothering her.

As if summoned, a loud knock sounded at the
door, startling her. She pulled the covers over her
head, ducked under the blankets, and then decided
not to be a coward.

"What is it?" she called out.

"Breakfast," he said in a deep, husky voice, which
she loved the sound of.

She sighed and pushed off the blankets, sitting up in bed and facing the door. "You can come in."

She made sure her long-sleeved pajamas were in place, ran her fingers through her loose hair, and hoped she looked okay to see him.

When the door opened, Zeus stepped in carrying a tray full of carefully laid out food. Her eyes widened as he walked over to the bed and set it down in front of her.

"Where's yours?" she asked.

"I already ate," he said.

She patted the bed, letting him know he could sit next to her, and after a moment's hesitation, he did so, looking wary. "I'm not going to bite," she said.

He gave her a dry grin and relaxed slightly. "Good to know." He looked too damn good in the morning. His dark hair was immaculately waved off his handsome face, which was freshly shaven. He wore a clean shirt in blue flannel that set off his gorgeous eyes, and his smooth, strong jaw made her want to run a hand along it.

But thinking of Zeus that way would just lead to more uncomfortable situations like last night. She fought back a scowl and reached for another pastry, biting into it just a little too intensely.

"Is something wrong?" Zeus asked, looking

confused.

"It's just… Never mind." She picked up some bacon, ate it, and washed it down with orange juice that tasted freshly squeezed.

He frowned, and she had the feeling that much stronger men had been intimidated by that intense gaze. She finished the eggs he'd made, hating to waste food, and then sat back against the headboard of the bed.

It was beautiful outside now that the sun had risen. She could see the light filtering through the endless green that surrounded the cabin. Despite living in a small mountain town, she'd never taken the time to go up and explore the wilderness around her, preferring to keep her head down and work. Now she thought maybe it had been a mistake.

"You like it?" he asked, tilting his head to study her, making that one lock of hair fall over his forehead.

"Like it?" she asked. "I love it. How much does one of these cabins run anyway? Maybe after I pay my debts, I can get something like this of my own."

A smile tilted one corner of his lips. "Maybe."

"So what did you do before you came here that made you such a badass?" she asked. "Oh, wait, you're not supposed to talk about it."

"No, sorry," he said, seeming genuinely apologetic that he couldn't share it with her.

"It's okay," she said, shrugging. "The past is the past. It makes us who we are, but I don't have to know it to get to know you."

He nodded and then laughed, a husky sound that made heat pool inside her. "I suppose. So what about your past, then? Before the boyfriend dragged you out here, I mean."

"Grew up not far from here. Another small town, more suburban. Not much to do, so I took jobs in local restaurants and such. Went to beauty school for a while, so if you ever want a haircut…"

He grinned and nodded. "Good to know."

It was amazing how comfortable he could make her feel just by asking questions and listening. "Anyway, I dropped out of beauty school because it was too expensive, and that's when I met Ben."

"Ben?"

"The ex who brought me out here."

"Oh," he said. She swore she could hear a slight growl in his voice.

"Anyway, that's me in a nutshell. I'm more interested in hearing about you. How did you end up in Bearstone Village?"

He shrugged his huge shoulders. "Ares was from

here. Said it was quiet. Good for people… like us."

"Like military?"

Something in his eyes was hesitant, and she got the feeling there was definitely a secret he was keeping from her. "Sure," he said. "Like military."

"Anyway, so you work with businesses here?"

"I fund them, yes. With the Devils in town, people need a fair loan sometimes."

"That's good of you. Most people would just run, seeing such a bad situation here."

"Not everyone can run," he said. "Some people have to stay. Besides, I like it here. The mountains bring me peace."

She nodded. She guessed peace was hard to find for a man like him, and it was beautiful up here.

"So anyway, that's me," he said. "What would you like to do today?"

She looked at him in surprise. "What do you mean? Don't we have to stay around here?"

"Well, yes. But there's plenty to do here. Hike, fish, go to the lake and sit."

"Is that safe?" she said.

"As long as you stay with me, it is," he said. "I'm protecting you, but I'm not going to keep you under lock and key."

"Good," she muttered, more to herself than to

him. "Because I'm not sure I can stay in this house with you much longer."

That had him sitting up, looking worried. And she had a feeling there wasn't much that worried this big man. "What do you mean? Am I doing something to bother you? Would you like me to leave?" He seemed genuinely concerned.

"No," she said, putting out a placating hand and then running it through her hair in exasperation. "No, it's just… nothing. You know what? Maybe a hike would be good," she said. "Some fresh air. I've never been up in these mountains."

And maybe the cold mountain air could cool her ardor for Zeus, make it easier to be around him.

He stood abruptly and strode from the room. When he came back, he was holding a box in his hands.

"What's that?" she asked, taking it from him.

"Hiking boots," he said. "To protect your feet."

"How do you have these?" she asked, looking inside. "They're just my size."

"I… um, I had Ares get some. I knew you might need something to walk around in up here."

"That was thoughtful of you," she said, touched once again by his unexpected kindness. His jaw tightened and he turned away, seemingly embarrassed.

"Anyway, I'll get a backpack ready and wait for you outside. Come out when you're changed." He was back to being brisk and effective, and he exited the door before she could say anything else.

She decided to quickly change. The sooner they left, the better.

* * *

Zeus eyed his mate as she scampered over a large boulder in their path and stood on top of it, looking around them. A part of him wanted to pull her down and enclose her in his arms where he knew she was safe. Another part of him knew they were alone in the mountains. His bear would sense anyone intruding on their space.

He was at home here, knew each part of the land like the back of his hand. He'd walked here many times, dealing with memories from the war or letting his bear run free or just trying to think of ways to approach and win over his mate.

It was surreal that she was here with him, but he still didn't know what to do with her. He just knew he needed to stay in control. Not come on too strong or too quickly and scare her away.

He'd almost messed it up last night when he'd been about to kiss her. But he'd known it was the wrong thing, that he should take it slowly and give her time. What kind of man would he be if he made things awkward for someone he was supposed to be protecting? She wasn't staying there because she liked him, but because she had nowhere else to go.

And she seemed a bit standoffish this morning, though he wasn't sure exactly what was wrong.

At least she was willing to let bygones be bygones as they explored the woods.

He was impressed by her simple wonder at the world around her. She seemed at home in the woods, entranced by them. They'd made their way up a long path above the cabin and were almost to the sparkling lake he wanted to show her.

His thinking place. And a great place to catch fish.

He supposed if the men he'd worked with saw him here, now, wondering how to woo a woman while scampering through the mountains, they'd never be able to believe it. He almost couldn't either.

He heard Carly gasp as she turned up ahead and the lake came into view, sparkling blue in the sunlight, surrounded on all sides by swaying trees.

"It's so gorgeous up here," she said. "How do

you keep it all to yourself?"

He didn't want to keep it all to himself. He wanted to share it with her. A vision came to him, him and Carly waking up together every morning, walking in the mountains, sitting by a campfire at night, and then going home to his cabin, curling up together...

He was instantly, achingly hard at the thought of it but pushed the thoughts away. All he had any right to focus on right now was making sure Carly was protected and happy. And crushing anyone who tried to threaten that.

She made her way to an overturned log and sat on it, watching the lake. Little ripples pushed by the wind shimmered silver in the light, and Zeus sighed as he stood behind his mate.

"I don't know how you don't just stay out here every day," she said contentedly.

"I do have to work sometimes, you know," he said.

"I know," she said. "Don't we all." She kicked at the soft soil in front of her and began to hum a little song.

She was beyond adorable, and the urge to take her in his arms became unbearable again, like it had been last night. She caught him watching her and gestured for him to join her on the log. He did so, careful not to sit too close.

As much as he sensed she wanted him, he didn't want to scare her off. He knew bears tended to be attractive to humans, and he wanted more than a simple fling with her. He wanted forever, and he was willing to wait for it.

"So you have any bears up here?" she asked, eyes twinkling.

"What?" he asked, heart thudding at the mention of bears. Was she saying…?

"Don't look so nervous. I just meant I know there are some up around Bearstone Park, but I hadn't heard of any being around here. Still, if there were, I think they would love this lake."

"There's only one around here," Zeus said carefully. "And he does seem to love this lake."

She sat up with wide eyes, suddenly looking around the clearing nervously. "Seriously? You've seen a bear around here and you still decided to bring me?"

Damn. That did sound stupid. And he couldn't really say, The bear is me. And any other bear that comes around you will get his throat torn out. Not yet. Not unless he wanted her to think he was crazy and run. He couldn't risk that while her life was threatened.

"I'd never let you be in danger," he said.

"You'd fight a bear for me?" she asked.

He nodded. He'd fight all the bears for her.

"Wow. You barely know me. I mean, I know we met a few times at the bar, but you never seemed to notice me."

She couldn't have been more wrong. Each time, he'd been waiting for the right moment to approach her, never knowing when that was. "I noticed you."

"Right," she said. "The fat waitress."

"The hot waitress." He grinned.

She growled in frustration and turned to him with irritation flashing in those pretty, light-brown eyes. "There you go again. Why do you keep saying things like that to me when you have no intentions on doing anything with me?"

He blinked, stunned. "I can't say you're attractive?"

"I don't want you to pity me or feel like you have to fluff my ego."

"I'm not," he said seriously, moving a little closer on the log. He couldn't resist reaching up and brushing her hair behind her ear so he could see her better. "I mean what I say."

"Sure," she said, scooting a little bit away. "Fine.

Just forget it." She ran her fingers through her hair as if trying to remove his touch, and the bear in him growled, wanting to put his mark all over his mate.

"I feel like you're mad again," he said. "I don't really get why."

She took a deep breath and then let it out in a small huff and glared at him. "Look, Zeus. I appreciate how nice you're being to me. And I know I told you I was insecure and you think you have to give me compliments even though you're not… you know… interested."

He stared at her in confusion. How could she think he wasn't interested? Clearly, he'd made a tactical error. One he meant to rectify.

"Like last night," she said. "If you say stuff like that, I'm going to misunderstand and then get disappointed when I… get ideas."

"Ideas about what?" he asked, moving closer still.

She moved back slightly, eyeing him warily. But he could feel the awareness of her body, her warmth, her scent. She wasn't afraid of him. She was aroused by him. "You know," she said, gesturing between them as she reached the edge of the log. "Ideas about us."

He moved forward, caging her in since she had nowhere to go. "What kind of ideas about us?"

She put her hands on his chest to keep him back. A bird sang overhead and wind rustled the trees above them. The fresh mountain air mingled with her scent in a heady mix that had him ready to take her back to the cabin, patience be damned.

"You know, you're an attractive man, and you're doing so much for me and saying nice things to me, and I start thinking…"

"Thinking what?" he pressed, leaning in closer so they were face to face, their lips nearly touching.

She leaned back slightly and lost her balance, nearly falling off the log, except his arm came around her back and held her up, pressed against him. He could feel her breath, see every flutter of her lashes. She was his. His.

"Thinking what?" he asked again.

She let out a shaky breath. "Thinking you want me."

He let out a low growl as his lips closed over hers, giving them both what they craved. The bear in him roared in approval. The man in him said he was going too fast. But if waiting was causing his mate to doubt him, then he wasn't going to wait anymore.

He'd let her know just how interested he was.

CHAPTER 6

Carly melted into Zeus's kiss, surrounded by his strong arms. Heat surged through her even as the cool mountain air surrounded them, making the scene that much more intense.

But before she could say anything, Zeus broke the kiss and stood up, swooping her up in his arms like she weighed nothing. She wrapped her arms around his neck and held on as he strode easily back down the path to the cabin.

"You don't have to carry me. You can—"

Another hard kiss from Zeus's soft, insistent lips silenced her protests and made her feel supported and loved in his arms. Somehow she got the feeling this was more than an attractive man kissing a woman. There seemed to be something beyond his kiss. A promise.

He pulled back, leaving her melted and pliant in his arms. She rested against his chest and couldn't wait to be inside the cabin with him, fulfilling all the promises she'd hoped for last night.

She'd never been the type of woman to move fast, but something about Zeus brought it out in her. She wanted to live on the wild side for once. She deserved a whirlwind romance with a mysterious, strong male who took care of everything.

She could deal with reality later.

When they reached the cabin, Zeus set her down to unlock the door and lock it behind them. Then he picked her up again, this time holding her under her thighs as she wrapped her legs around his waist, and they kissed all the way into the bedroom. He pulled away from her mouth to kiss her neck, her shoulders, her sensitive ears. She growled in approval and held him tight, not wanting to give him any chance to stop pleasing her.

When they reached the bedroom, he set her down in front of the bed, and when he reached down for another kiss, she planted her hands on his chest and pushed him hard so he fell back onto the bed. He went along with it easily, and she followed him onto the mattress and straddled him, caught up in an animalistic lust she'd didn't even fully understand.

He was hot, he was hers, and she loved the hard feel of his thighs under her, the sensual search of his rough hands over her body.

What they were doing couldn't be taken back, but Carly didn't care. She just knew she wanted this man more badly than air itself, and if she didn't take him now, she knew she'd always regret it.

Zeus wrapped his arms around her and pressed her body against him, surrounding her with his hard, solid strength. His hands ran down her soft, curvy sides and squeezed her hips lightly, sending shivers down her back and making her feel utterly beautiful in his eyes.

"You're so gorgeous, Carly. More beautiful than anyone else in the entire world," Zeus said between kisses, his voice low and husky.

It seemed unbelievable that this man she'd barely met could be saying this to her. But by the way he kissed her, the way he looked at her, she had to believe him. At least for now.

"If you want me, then show me," Carly said, arching against him as he growled with approval. He kissed just below her ear, making her gasp with arousal. He trailed rough kisses up along her neck, each one a small spark of electricity that turned her on more with each touch.

His hands felt amazing at her sides, teasing and stroking just under her breasts. She pulled her shirt off in one easy motion, leaving her bared to him in her bra and jeans only.

Zeus smiled in approval, a wicked flash of white teeth that was so unlike the shy man he'd shown her so far. This was the badass under the surface, the part of him he kept hidden that she'd always sensed was there. The thought heated her even further.

Zeus cupped her breasts in her bra, rubbing his thumbs deftly over her nipples, and then reached around and unhooked it with an easy flick. Then he leaned forward, placing a long, heated kiss on each one.

She'd never been loved like this before. Never had a man so focused on her pleasure and her curves, and she savored it.

"So perfect," he said reverently, licking each nipple as an ache rose inside her.

She wanted him. She wanted him so much she couldn't see straight. She couldn't respond, so she just held on to his shoulders as he brought his hands down to massage and squeeze as his lips found hers again, taking her more deeply this time, his tongue sweeping inside to own her completely.

His hands found her nipples again, and she arched back at the powerful sensation, loving how he somehow knew exactly what she needed and how to give it to her.

One hand reached down to her ass and squeezed gently, then a little harder, pulling her closer against him. She could feel his firm length and hunger shot up inside her. She wanted him filling her, taking her like no one ever had or ever could.

"You want me?" he asked huskily, a statement as much as a question.

"Yes," she said.

"You're sure," he said.

"Yes," she answered, digging her hands into his hair as his head found her nipples again, teasing and licking as his fingers toyed with the edge of her jeans.

"There's no going back after this," he said. "You're mine."

She nodded against him eagerly. She'd say anything, anything, right now to get him inside her.

He lifted her off of him and knelt above her on the bed, pulling her jeans down over her curves slowly, easily stripping her of her clothing. After staring hungrily down at her panties, he reached down and ripped them off in one quick, painless movement that had her gasping at how dominant he was.

He came over her, hands on either side, and took her mouth again. "Mine," he whispered, his lips teasing hers.

"Yours," she said, licking his bottom lip and drawing a growl from him.

He stood and pulled off his shirt, revealing perfect, huge muscles lightly sheened with sweat, and then reached for his jeans, watching her eyes. She let him see her bare hunger, and his eyes flashed in approval just before he removed his pants, leaving him exposed to her.

Damn, he went commando. Of course he did.

He pulled out a condom, rolled it over himself, and was on her the next second. His hard body covered hers, his muscles bunched as he held himself over her, and he stroked her hair for a second before taking her in another hard kiss. She was so wet for him, and when he reached down with a hand to test her, he growled in approval before stroking hungrily over her folds, finding the spot that pleasured her most.

She arched back with a gasp, writhing under his huge body. His massive chest pressed against her as he stroked and played, and she had no choice but to lie there and accept the pleasure as it continued to build inside her. Coiling tighter and tighter, rising higher and higher. His deft fingers focused as his blue eyes studied her face, eager for her pleasure.

Then she went, gasping for air as pleasure unlike anything she'd felt surged through her, fresh as mountain air, overwhelming as being submerged in an icy lake. It felt like she was coming alive for the first time in so long, and as wave after wave of release burst through her, she clung to him and called his name. Zeus, Zeus, Zeus.

As she finished, she looked up into his hungry eyes, panting for breath. That had felt wonderful, but she was far from done.

"More," she said, wrapping her arms around him and holding him close. "Give me all of you."

"You already have it," he said hoarsely, and then the next moment, he pushed inside her in one smooth thrust that had her bursting with sensation, filled more completely than ever before.

She writhed against him, trying to adjust, trying to comprehend the pleasure bursting inside her, the anticipation of something amazing that was on the way. His arms trembled slightly as he stayed carefully still, making sure she was okay. She let him see the bare hunger in her eyes and saw it reflected back at her. Whatever this feeling was, whatever was happening between them, he was lost to it too. And as she reached her arms around him and dug her nails into his back, he began to move.

And it felt unlike anything in the universe. "Don't stop," she said, wrapping her legs around his waist to keep him close. "Don't ever stop."

He growled against her neck and kept going, moving them both toward a destination that felt as exciting as it was inevitable. She'd never felt like this with a man, never known it was possible, and she still didn't know if it was possible with anyone but the man inside her.

It didn't matter. All that mattered was that he kept moving, stroking steadily with his hard length as sparks shot through her with an incredible intensity, building a pressure inside her unlike anything she'd ever known. As he moved faster, she cried out with each thrust, holding him with all of her, stroking him with all of her, feeling how perfectly they fit together.

And as his breathing increased and she realized he was close, she felt her own body start to tip over the edge, ready to fall into something incredible. Then an explosion of light burst through her, flooding her body with a pleasure that was indescribable and almost too strong. She held Zeus's shoulders and screamed, at the same time she heard him utter her name in a hoarse oath and go still against her, jerking inside her and stroking her through her orgasm. It was heaven—more than heaven—and she still couldn't believe it was happening.

She held him close through the almost scary, foreign sensation and wondered how she'd gotten so lucky, how fate had brought her here at the right moment with the right man. He held her tight, staying with her every moment as they finished their release together.

And then after, he held her close as endorphins flooded her, keeping her in a fantasy state where everything felt just perfect. She wrapped her arms around him and sighed, waiting for her heart rate to return to normal. She could still feel him inside her. Still feel the warmth of his body, the intensity of his thrusts as he took her. Still feel the hard possessiveness of his movements.

As her body stayed near his and refused to calm down, she decided not to overthink what had happened. It had been wonderful and more than she'd ever expected, and no matter what happened between her and Zeus in the future, she'd never regret what they'd just done.

In fact, she hoped they did it again soon.

* * *

Zeus was wracked with guilt as he held his mate in his arms. Holding her had been the most pleasurable experience of his life, but he'd damn near taken her without protection, damn near completed the first part of claiming her as mate. The second part was telling her about his bear and letting her accept it, and he wasn't willing to risk that yet.

It'd been the hardest thing he'd ever done to hold back, to give her pleasure but resist taking her. As he'd stroked inside her hot warmth, looked into her beautiful eyes, he'd wanted nothing more than to ensure she was his forever.

But it was too early, and if all Carly wanted from him was pleasure without assurances, that's what he would give. He knew her last relationship had been bad, and maybe this was her way of exploring things without going any further.

Nonetheless, he knew she didn't have the feelings for him that he had for her. That he'd had for months.

She'd said she was his, but that was in the depths of passion and couldn't mean to her what it had to him.

To her, he was an attractive man who was kind. To him, she was everything. He kissed the top of her head and tried not to think about his predicament. But the soldier in him wanted a plan, wanted to know the next step in the battle to win Carly's heart.

But he didn't know. He'd never fought a battle like that before. He'd never wanted to win so badly.

He kept his arms tight around her, glad she seemed happy to snuggle against him. He uttered nothing, worried anything he said would give him away. He'd already blurted out things during sex that probably sounded too intense, if she'd really been able to think about them.

He'd been caught up in the moment, in a pleasure he hadn't known existed. Being with his mate in general was a kind of peace this weary soldier had never thought he'd experience. But making love to her, being inside her, that was coming home.

She rested in his arms, her breathing returning to normal, her curves going soft against him as she stretched out in front of him. He spooned her from behind, loving how her body curved in front of him. He could sense she was quietly thinking, and he would have given anything to be able to hear her thoughts at that moment, to know what she wanted from him or what exactly he could do to make her his forever.

Instead, he pressed his lips to her hair again, loving the softness of it, the sweet smell of female. His bear purred in contentment, and she laughed, snuggling against him.

"What's that sound?" she asked.

"Nothing," he said quickly, pulling her close.

She laughed and pushed against him, sitting up to look at him. Her bare breasts glowed and her soft skin tantalized him. Even though he'd just taken her, his body already begged to do it again.

She put a hand over her breasts with a self-conscious smile and stifled a giggle. "Are you hungry?" she asked. "It sounds like your stomach's growling."

"Yes, I'm hungry," he said, eyeing her.

She chuckled and pulled the covers up against her, looking shy. The moment stretched between them, a tension he couldn't really understand. But they'd just made love, and that had changed everything.

The sound of his alarm going off jerked him unpleasantly from the little world they'd been sharing, far from gangs or danger or death.

He covered her with blankets and stood, pulling on his jeans as he crept stealthily to the door.

Someone had breached the perimeter. He had a small hope it was Ares, but he wasn't taking any chances, not with his mate here and vulnerable.

"Stay here. I'll be back," he said.

She nodded quietly, and he loved the confidence in her eyes as she watched him go. His mate trusted him to protect her. And luckily, thanks to his past as a soldier, he knew that trust wasn't misplaced.

There was no one in the world that could take her away from him. Not without the fight of a lifetime.

CHAPTER 7

Zeus ran down to the first floor, checking his phone for additional information.

It had alerted him of the initial breach a couple minutes ago. Zeus swore to himself. He should have been paying more attention. The alarm in the house only went off if he ignored the initial warnings, so whatever was outside had already been there for a few minutes.

He hoped Ares really was just a numbskull who always forgot to deactivate the alarm. But as Zeus came to up to the door, he opened a small closet to his right, slipped on his boots, and pulled out a leather vest that he kept hung there that held a few helpful things.

Just in case.

Zeus slowly pushed open the front door but didn't come outside. He listened for sounds coming from the forest, scented the varying smells that wafted toward him on the afternoon breeze. Pine needles. Bark. Aspen logs.

And something else.

Zeus quietly stepped out onto the porch, every muscle tensed, ready for action.

From his right, he heard movement and turned quickly to face three large men charging directly at him, brandishing knives.

In an instant, Zeus's mind and body sprang into action. Putting years of sparring and military hand-to-hand combat to use, coupled with his supernatural bear strength, he engaged the three of them at once.

He grabbed the outstretched hand of the lead man and flung him backward. Then, with one swift kick of his steel-toed boot, he struck the hand of the man on his right, sending his large knife clattering to the side. The man backed off, nursing his now-broken wrist. Zeus rushed toward the last man, passing his swinging knife and catching the man's arm in a vise between his chest and elbow. For a moment, the man looked at Zeus wide-eyed in shock, right before Zeus pulled the man's face forward into a ferocious head-butt, knocking the man backward and toppling over the railing of the deck onto the dirt.

As he fought, Zeus heard engines roar to life nearby. He came back to the man with the broken hand and knocked him out with a swift hook to the jaw, just in time to see motorcycles coming over the road leading into the clearing, whooping and firing their guns into the air and at him.

The sounds of the gunshots rang through the forest, and Zeus rolled behind a wood pillar at the corner of the porch out of the line of fire. He brandished a compact pistol stowed in the left pocket of his vest and pulled the slide to chamber a round.

"We're here for the girl. We know you got her inside!" one man yelled as the bikes drove up to the front of the house and waited.

Zeus wondered how it was they'd found him out here. And even if they did find out, he'd never thought the Red Devils would try to come this far from their home turf, even for Carly.

If they wanted to bring the war to his doorstep, then he was more than willing to oblige. Anytime.

"Give up now and we promise not to kill ya!" shouted another. As he did, several men came off their bikes and took cover in the underbrush at the edge of the clearing. They were armed. They were ready.

They were about to get their asses kicked.

Zeus looked over his shoulder and saw about ten bikers waiting at the front of the house, engines idling. He guessed there was probably three or four more in the thick ferns and brush that surrounded the house as well.

"Do you accept the terms of your surrender?" the lead man asked Zeus. He wore a red and black bandana and had a large, polished chopper of a motorcycle.

Zeus wasn't up for negotiations. He turned over his left shoulder, aimed down the sights of his .45, and fired one shot at the leader, dropping him to the ground.

"Consider that my surrender," Zeus called to the stunned group of men.

In an instant, the forest exploded with sound. The men swore unspeakable things and revved their engines, circling around the house. Zeus knew he was too exposed here on the deck, and he needed to draw fire away from the cabin to protect Carly. So he leapt over the side railing and rolled to the ground, coming onto his feet and bolting for the nearest patch of trees. All around him, he could hear bullets whizzing past and engines screaming as they approached.

As Zeus ran, he aimed and shot the front tire of one of the bikes as it zoomed toward him, and it veered out of control and careened into the forest with its rider. Just as another swiped past him, he slid beneath a large fern and ducked behind a tree.

Using his newfound cover, he fired on two men sprinting up the stairs and heading into the house. Both men slumped over before they could reach the door.

So long as Zeus fought, nobody would ever come near his mate. He'd make sure of that.

More shots ricocheted around him, and Zeus ducked behind another tree. As much as he wanted to go into the clearing, guns blazing, he knew he had neither the ammo nor the manpower to do so. And the last thing his mate needed was a dead protector.

To his right, one of the men that earlier had disappeared into the tree line came toward him, not knowing Zeus was hidden there. Hoping to conserve his ammunition, Zeus pulled a throwing knife and hurled it toward the man, hitting him square in the chest. The goon yelped and dropped to the ground.

Zeus hurried to where he fell and grabbed the scuffed, worn-looking pistol on the ground near his body. Though it didn't look like the most reliable weapon, two was better than one.

Welding both firearms, Zeus fired on the circle of moving bikes, aiming for tires, engines, gas tanks, and the riders themselves. Though his accuracy certainly would have been better with only one gun, Zeus knew he needed to cull their numbers quickly in case they had reinforcements on the way.

No matter how unlikely it was, Zeus always planned for the worst.

Immediately, bikes began overturning and riders fell to the ground. Those that weren't flung from their bikes or shot down quickly got the picture and dismounted, scattering for the road. Zeus fired off the last rounds in both pistols and went back into cover, discarding the thug's pistol and putting a fresh magazine in his own gun. Out of the corner of his eye, he saw another man making for the house and shot him down.

A split second after that happened, Zeus heard a loud pop across the clearing and felt searing pain rip into his side. Instinctively, he went prone and rolled behind a tree, out of the line of fire, before whoever was shooting got another chance.

Now on his back, Zeus looked over his body and saw blood welling up on his side.

Shit, he was hit.

He quickly lifted his shirt and checked the

wound. It had grazed his ribs, leaving a deep gash. It wasn't the worst wound he'd had, not even close. And thanks to his bear strength and the incredible healing power all shifters had, he knew his body could take it. But the dangerous thing was that it hadn't been from something like a handgun. Based on the size of the wound and just how damn bad it hurt, the shot had been from a much higher velocity weapon, like a hunting or assault rifle.

At first glance, Zeus hadn't seen anyone with anything bigger than a handgun. And just based on their ragtag tactics, he didn't expect any of them to be terribly accurate. But someone had been able to hit him from somewhere across the clearing and with surprising accuracy.

Zeus was just getting started. To anyone else, that shot would have likely been lethal. But there was one thing none of the men out there knew and he did.

There was another fighter inside him, one stronger than they could handle. He felt his body change and let out a roar as he charged into the clearing.

They'd threatened his mate and woken the animal inside him.

Now they'd have to deal with the big, bad bear.

* * *

Carly watched in terror at the melee below. From the bedroom window, she could see Zeus as he ran for the trees and fought the intruders from there.

Yesterday, when Zeus had protected her in the bar, she'd seen just how capable and strong he really was. And how protective. And since then, she'd learned snippets here and there from Ares or from himself about his past in the military, apparently doing something he didn't or couldn't talk about.

But seeing him out there, singlehandedly fighting what looked like twenty or so men, fearlessly and all by himself, Carly knew for certain that Zeus had seen combat in his previous life. Lots of it.

Even though he took cover right at the edge of the clearing of trees, Carly could make out Zeus's huge figure as it dodged, rolled, returned fire, and moved effortlessly through the shrubs, fighting what seemed like an endless onslaught of men.

Her heart sank at the thought of anything happening to him at all, and she thought momentarily about surrendering if that meant they would let him live. But considering just how ferociously he was fighting them, she didn't think it was something Zeus would ever agree with.

Part of her cursed her luck for having had the

run-in with the Red Devils back at the bar. But she also knew if it hadn't have happened, she probably wouldn't have been brought up here to this beautiful forest and been able to have the most mind-blowing sex with the hottest man she'd ever known.

The fighting was starting to dwindle, when she heard a loud shot ring through the forest. Zeus staggered and disappeared from her view suddenly.

Was he okay? Had he been shot?

Carly's heart raced. She picked up her cellphone to call 9-1-1. However, when she unlocked it and started to dial, she heard several loud beeps, then nothing. She checked her phone and saw a small "no service" in the top left corner. Dammit, she didn't have service this high in the mountains, and until now, she hadn't bothered to check. And from what she'd seen in the house, she didn't recall Zeus having any landline. All she could do was wait, eyes focused on the last spot she'd seen him.

What would happen if the Red Devils did get their hands on her?

She tried to put away the horrible possibilities that ensued from the thought and silently hoped for the best.

By now, those who were still left standing started to pull fallen comrades out of the clearing to the side, while others approached his last-seen position, guns trained on the thicket of ferns and brush.

Out of nowhere, a long, loud roar reverberated through the forest around them, shaking Carly to her core. It was unlike any sound she'd ever heard before. Looking down at the thugs, she saw them exchange harried looks before moving forward again.

A split second later, a huge brown grizzly charged out of the forest and gave another ferocious roar that made the walls of the house shake, then charged at the men. Some of them froze in their place, dropping their guns at their sides. Others turned and ran for dear life, bolting for the nearest motorcycle and running for the trees behind them.

Carly felt herself freeze as well at the sight of the larger-than-life creature. She'd seen a few bears at a zoo when she was little, but this one seemed bigger than anything she could have imagined.

And where was Zeus? Was he still okay?

To her surprise, the bear was not only huge, but it was fast as well. With one swipe, a biker was thrown twenty feet into the forest, out of Carly's view. A moment later, the bear grabbed a motorcycle in its mouth and hurled it toward another man about to shoot at it, knocking him over. Some of men regrouped and fired their weapons at the bear, but it seemed to have the same effect a BB gun would on a raging bull.

None.

Carly remembered the bear Zeus had mentioned before when they were at the lake. Was this it? The thought that Zeus lived so close to such a merciless, gigantic killing machine was unsettling, even though he hadn't sounded worried at all about the creature when he brought up the subject earlier. When she saw Zeus again, she would have to talk to him about it.

Roaring and clawing, the bear made its way through the clearing and into the forest, where she saw it chasing several men who had been hiding there. By the time it reached them, they'd gone out of her view from the small bedroom window, and Carly scanned the forest for where she'd seen Zeus.

Carly heard one last roar and saw the bear charge back into the forest from where it had first come from, overturning the brush and disappearing behind the trees in a matter of seconds. She marveled at how close the creature had come to where Zeus had been, but from what she'd seen, it had gone right past him. Maybe Zeus had seen the bear and hid in the thicket, out of sight?

The clearing was quiet, aside from the quickly

waning sounds of a few motorcycles carrying men that had managed to escape in time. But those too soon faded, leaving just the sight of mangled motorcycles and unconscious or dead gangsters.

Carly's heart stopped when Zeus didn't appear. Should she go outside and look for him? She turned the thought over and over in her mind. There was still a risk in her going outside. But it was also possible he could be out there, bleeding and dying, right now, and without help, he could surely be doomed.

She couldn't bear the thought of losing Zeus, only now when she'd just found him. She grabbed a pair of sandals from her bag and threw on her jacket, going to the window to look one last time before running outside.

To her surprise, she saw Zeus, shirtless and shoeless, walking across the clearing toward the house. His left arm hung limp, weakly holding a gun in his hand, with his right hand pressing what looked like a torn piece of fabric to his left chest. She could see blood running down his abdomen from what must have been a gunshot wound he was covering.

Carly didn't care about the danger. Zeus was hurt. She ran for the stairs, going down them by twos and threes, and swung open the front door. When she did, Zeus looked up at her and smiled weakly, his dark haired mussed and his body riddled with cuts and scrapes. He walked more quickly, and when she reached him, she threw her arms around him, glad to know he was still alive.

"Are you okay? You're injured," Carly said, holding back tears.

"I'm fine for now. Let's get inside, quick. There might be more out there," Zeus whispered, his voice strained. Even like this, just the sound of his voice reassured her that everything was going to be okay, somehow.

Carly went with him as they walked inside and closed the door. She locked it while Zeus called Ares, informing him of the situation and telling him to come quickly. As they waited, Zeus went to work cleansing the gunshot wound and patching it up. To her surprise, the bleeding had already stopped by the time it was bandaged, but when she asked, Zeus just said it had been a clean shot and it only grazed him.

Faster than she would have guessed, Ares came roaring up the mountain in his truck. He strode into the house, carrying what looked like an arsenal of weaponry in a large, black bag, and started to unpack, when Zeus spoke.

"Sorry, Ares, not today. We just need to get out

of here quickly. Can we stay at your place tonight?"

Ares halted his unpacking. "Of course. Anything for you, boss," he said.

"Thanks. Carly, you go get your things together while I grab a few necessities. Ares, wait in the car for us," Zeus said in his commanding voice. Second by second, he seemed to be getting better, from what she could tell, though maybe Zeus was just so focused right now that he could ignore the pain from the injury.

Carly ran upstairs and gathered her stuff. Thankfully, she hadn't taken much out since last night when it had been brought to her in the first place, and in less than a minute, she was back downstairs, ready to go.

Zeus had a backpack and one large suitcase and was standing by the door, waiting for her.

"Emergency kit, for situations when I need to leave in a hurry," he said, ushering her through the door and out to Ares's large black truck. Zeus tossed their things in the back and opened the passenger door, helping Carly get in before getting in the backseat of the cab.

When they reached town, Ares called 9-1-1 so the police and paramedics could make their way up and tend to the wounded. After a few more minutes of driving, they arrived at a surprisingly large house surrounded by a tall, concrete barrier with a metal gate. With the press of a button, Ares pulled into a private driveway and closed the gate behind them.

They were safe. For now.

CHAPTER 8

They got out of the car quietly. Ares carried the bags and led the way up his drive and toward the house, which was tall and foreboding, with no decorative frills. Probably two stories high, made of solid concrete, reinforced windows. It definitely stood out in the small town, or would if anyone had the guts to look over the huge concrete barrier that surrounded it.

Ares unlocked and opened the door, and Carly gasped at the difference in the interior. Pure luxury, from the beautiful rugs to the hand-carved furniture that looked much like the stuff in Zeus's cabin. It made sense, since Zeus had told Carly Ares constructed the furniture.

Right now, she was just grateful Ares had been

able to come and help. She was in awe of the way he called Zeus boss and had said he'd do anything for him. Clearly, there was still a lot to learn about the man she was falling in love with.

That's right. She was already falling in love with him. From the moment he'd touched her, back on their walk in the woods, she'd realized something powerful and dangerous was forming between them. Something she wanted to keep exploring. But first, she had to make sure Zeus was okay.

Ares tried to help him to the nearest couch, but Zeus pulled away, walking on his own to a hard, wooden chair.

"I'm fine," he said wearily, slumping into it. "I don't want to get blood on your couch."

"Fuck it. I can buy another," Ares said, sitting down and running a hand through his ruffled blond hair. His bag of weaponry sat beside him, making Carly slightly nervous.

"Can you put those back in the safe?" Zeus asked with a raised eyebrow. "They're making Carly nervous."

"No, it's okay—" she said.

But Ares had already nodded and was walking away in the direction of the doorway. Zeus gave her a tired smile, looking her over as if making sure she was okay, when he was the one who was injured.

She walked over to him and reached for his shirt, but he caught her hand and lifted it to his lips, kissing it slowly in a way that sent heat sizzling through her. Still, she pulled back and gave him a frown. "I need to look at your wound. I'm worried about it."

"I'm fine," he said. "I heal quick."

"You were shot," she said. "I don't understand why you won't let me look at it and help you. I've stitched up my brother before when he fell."

"I'm afraid this is different," Ares said, cutting into their conversation as she struggled with Zeus to try and see his injury. Stubborn man was going to get an infection if he didn't let someone take a look at it. Ares put a hand on her shoulder and pulled her back. "I got it, sweetness," he said gently, and she stepped aside.

Zeus let out a low growl, and Ares laughed, kneeling in front of him. "Cool it, big guy. You know I call all women sweetness."

"Not Carly," he said.

"Yeah, yeah, I get it, boss," Ares said, lifting his shirt and blocking her view of the wound. He let out a low whistle. "He's gonna be fine. Just a flesh wound."

"Doesn't he need stitches? It was bleeding so bad

before."

Ares shook his head and lowered the shirt, gazing at her calmly.

She stomped a foot. "I don't care how macho you military men think you are. Someone needs to disinfect that thing or he's going to get an infection."

Ares and Zeus looked at each other in puzzlement, and Ares sighed. "All right. But I'll do it when you're out of the room. Zeus here doesn't want you to see it."

"Why, because you think I can't handle it? I want to help."

Zeus's calm blue eyes met hers. "Carly. Please."

She was angry. Angry that he was hurt, angry that he was keeping her away when all of this was because of her and she desperately felt like she needed to do something for him in return. Angry at being closed off by the two large men. Angry that Ares knew all of Zeus's secrets and she was barely scratching his surface. Seeing how he fought in the clearing before he went down, she was certain his whole life had been about war until he came to Bearstone Village.

But now wasn't the time to talk about it, and she would respect his need for privacy. Whatever the reason.

"All right," she said. "But call me back when

you're done." In the meantime, she'd go find a quiet place to sit and try not to think about the man she was coming to love running into a hailstorm of bullets and limping away bleeding and hurting.

* * *

When Carly was gone, Ares grabbed wipes from a first aid kit to clean the mostly healed wound. "That was risky, you know," he said, looking into Zeus's eyes as he wiped away the blood. "You should have waited for me to come over," Ares said.

"It was too late," Zeus replied. "They would have breached the house. I had to protect Carly." He let Ares put a bandage over the area, just so Carly would be convinced he was fine, and then pulled his shirt down and let out a harsh breath.

"You want to change?" Ares asked. "Or want to go over it now? I want to know everything that happened, from the perimeter breach to when I showed up and everyone was down."

Zeus sighed. "Damn, I'm tired. I haven't taken on that many men in a long time, amateur or not."

Ares's lips quirked in a smile. "Looks like a dozen men are still no match for our Zeus."

"More than a dozen," Zeus said, and the two

men shared a cocky grin that most people would never understand. But Zeus had protected what was his. That's all that mattered.

"So what were you doing that you didn't notice the initial perimeter breach?"

Zeus felt blood rush into his neck and avoided Ares's piercing gaze. The other man's green eyes were unnervingly adept at reading between the lines. "Ah, hell," he said. "It wasn't very late. I just didn't hear the initial beep on my phone. Even if I had, the result would have been the same."

A slow grin spread over Ares's face, and Zeus gave him a shove. "Stop thinking about it," he said, and Ares raised his hands in surrender.

"All right, boss, not thinking about it," he said.

"What are you not thinking about?" Carly asked, appearing in the doorway.

"Nothing," Ares said, stretching out on the couch as Zeus settled back into his chair.

He was proud of how she'd handled the situation. She'd stayed out of danger but been ready and waiting for him. Worried for him. She'd feared for his safety, not only her own. And she'd been fiercely protective when she thought he was wounded.

It was all he could ask for in a mate. His bear had chosen wisely.

His bear had also kicked ass.

Zeus gave Ares all the info he could while trying not to look at Carly as she sat on the couch a little ways from Ares. She was so perfect, her brown hair mussed and fluffy, but so soft, her whiskey eyes glittering with emotion as they relived the event. Her rosy lips were pursed as she listened to their thoughts on the matter.

He wanted to just pick her up and take her back to the bedroom and cuddle her until he convinced the animal inside him she was okay. But he had to take care of business first.

"So then I was wounded, and then…" He looked at Carly, wondering how to handle the bear thing. Had she seen?

"Then a big freaking bear came out of the woods and messed everyone up," Carly said, shaking her head. "I know you two aren't going to believe me, but it's all I've been thinking about… you know, when not thinking about the fight and Zeus getting hurt. I mean, Zeus said there was a bear up in the woods, but I didn't think it was friendly to humans." She put her head in her hands. "Now that I think about it, it's almost like he was protecting us. I mean, he fought like a demon but never threatened or hurt Zeus."

Ares's eyes twinkled as he looked over at Zeus, and Zeus sent him a warning glare. "Now that you mention it, Zeus did say there was a bear up around his place. A friendly one, though," Ares said.

Carly raised an eyebrow. "Are bears ever friendly? I thought they ate campers and stuff."

Ares grimaced in disgust. "None of the bears I know."

She raised an eyebrow. "And you know a lot of bears?"

Ares didn't miss a beat. "Well, yeah. I grew up in Bearstone Village. Worked summers in Bearstone Park. There are bears around."

"I see," she said. "Why do I feel like there's something you two aren't telling me?" She glared at Zeus, and he looked away, not meeting her gaze. He could tell her when all of this cooled down. It would be too much right now.

"Anyway, this bear up around Zeus's place, what did he do?"

She laughed, shaking her head as she remembered it. "I don't know. He knocked them off their motorcycles, stuff like that."

"Sounds like a badass bear," Ares said, grinning.

"But was I hallucinating due to stress?" Carly asked, looking like she was doubting herself. "I mean, why would a bear join a fight?"

Ares's eyes were doing that twinkling thing again, though his voice was serious. "Maybe it was protecting its territory. Bears are very possessive of what's theirs."

"Yeah," Zeus said, joining in with a gruff voice. "That bear especially."

Carly looked between them in puzzlement and then laughed. "Well, I'm just glad you're okay and the bear was on the side of justice."

"Always," Zeus said, unable to help himself. "But just in case, probably don't trust any other bears."

She waved a hand. "Of course not. Honestly, bears terrify me. I'm not even sure I'd feel safe going back to your cabin, knowing that one's going to be around."

Zeus tried not to frown. He knew Carly didn't know anything about shifters, and bears were naturally scary animals, but part of him was still hurt by that. It made him that much more reluctant to tell her the truth. Could he really hope she would accept him when he did?

"Hey now," Ares said. "Bears are just like any creatures, including humans. There are some bad ones and some good ones, but most of them won't hurt you unless you try to hurt them or their family."

Carly sighed and nodded. "I suppose." She walked over to Zeus and put a warm, soft hand on his shoulder, calming the animal inside him. She might not know what he was, but for now, she made him feel at peace, at home. Made the animal inside him purr.

He had to hope she would accept him when the time came. He had to trust his bear knew best.

He turned to Ares. "So what now?"

Ares stood. "I'm going out to catch up with the police at the scene, if they're still there. You know they're slow to respond. If they ask about you two, I'll tell them you disappeared into the woods. Make them waste some time sending a search party. That way they'll be on the wrong trail."

Zeus nodded. "That gives us time to make plans on how to deal with the Devils in the meantime."

"Right," Ares agreed, stretching his shoulders, cracking his neck, and heading out.

"You armed?" Zeus asked.

Ares let out a huge grin that would have looked movie-star bright if it didn't seem so predatory. "Abso-fuckin-lutely."

Zeus nodded. "Good."

"You okay staying here with your lady?" Ares asked.

"Of course," Zeus said. "When will you be back?"

"I plan to be out all night, most of the morning. If I come back here, they'll assume you're here. You know how the security works. No one is getting in without alerting you, and you know where the safe room is."

Zeus did. He stood with some effort, and he and Ares did a quick shoulder clapping hug before Ares gave them a mock salute and left, leaving Zeus alone with Carly.

CHAPTER 9

She looked him over. "We should get you changed," she said. "Come on. Let's find you some clothes."

He nodded and was amused when she came to him and put a hand around his waist, as if her short, curvy frame could support him. Still, to humor her, and because he liked her touch, he let her walk with him down the hall. He gestured to the guest bedroom that Ares kept ready for him when he came into town, and she walked in with him and made him sit on the bed.

"There are clothes in the closet," he said. "I sometimes stay here with Ares when I'm in town."

"What do you come to town for anyway?" she asked, blushing slightly as she pulled some things out of the closet and laid them out on the bed. Her blush deepened as she reached for the hem of his shirt, and he raised his arms to make it easy for her to pull it over his head.

He was tired, but not too tired to be totally turned on by his mate removing his clothing. When she reached for the button of his jeans, he gently moved her hand away. "I got it," he said, not wanting her to undo his pants and see just how affected he was at a time when he shouldn't be thinking of it.

She reluctantly turned away with a sigh. "I like helping you, you know. I just… I know I'm not a badass like you or Ares. But don't shut me out. Let me help. You know?"

He was stunned. He quickly pulled on his shirt and changed his jeans as he dealt with what she'd just said.

He hadn't expected her to be hurt by him not letting her check out a bloody wound or undo his pants and have to see his raging boner brought on just by being in her presence. He still felt like the luckiest man in the world just to be near her. He didn't want to do anything that put her off of him.

He and Ares had to get her out of the room so she didn't see how quickly his wound had healed. Revealing yourself as a shifter to a human who hadn't agreed to mate you was forbidden and carried serious consequences, up to and including brainwashing and death. He'd only been trying to protect her.

But he supposed he wouldn't have liked to be sent away when she was hurt either.

"I'm sorry," he said. "I've been on my own a long time. I don't want to bother you."

"You saved my life. Twice now. Don't you get that I want to care for you too?"

Zeus was silent. No, he didn't get that. His job was to protect her and take care of everything. Her job was to be happy and safe. And how could a sweet, friendly woman like her care about a wounded, grumpy warrior like him? Sure, he could take down a dozen men with his bare hands, but that didn't mean he deserved her love or respect. He had to earn it.

She sat next to him and reached over, playing with the button on his jeans as he felt the blood in his body move to a specific, inconvenient location. "I get you're a big, bad fighter. I get I can't charge into battle with you. But it was terrifying being in there, having to stand back and watch, knowing there was nothing I could do, even call the police."

She shuddered, and he wrapped an arm around her, holding her tight. "No, you don't have to comfort me," she said, starting to pull away but giving up when he insisted on keeping her close. "It's just that when you're done with that fight, the least I can do is take care of you."

"I don't fight so you'll owe me something in return," he said.

"Why do you fight, then?"

He eyed her quietly. "Because it's the right thing." Because I love you. But he couldn't say that.

She looked slightly disappointed with his answer, and he wished he could take it back. But then she brightened. "You're a good man, Zeus."

"Thanks," he said. Her words meant more to him than she could have known.

Despite how tired he was from the fight, he ached to claim his mate. Ached to hold her after the battle and remind himself of what he'd won, what he'd protected.

But he needed to save his strength. They might have to fight again soon. He touched her cheek gently, and she flushed and snuggled against his hand, making him melt inside. There would be plenty of time to please his mate later, after he'd ended every man who tried to come between them.

"I don't know what it is," she said. "We barely know each other, but you make me feel more treasured than anyone has in my life."

That was because she meant more to him than anyone ever had or would. But it ached that he couldn't say it yet. Still, he could say some things.

"You asked why I came into town. I didn't answer. The truth is I could do most of my business from my computer at home or on my phone. But there was one thing I couldn't do at home."

"Oh yeah?" she asked. "What's that?"

"See you," he admitted.

Her eyes widened as she tilted her head up at him. "What do you mean? You came to the bar to see me?"

He nodded.

"Every time?"

He nodded again, glad any embarrassment he felt didn't show. He wasn't a hardened warrior for nothing.

"That's..." She bit her lip and gave him a small smile that heated him down to his toes and made his pants even tighter. "That's actually really sweet. I always liked seeing you. Unlike some of the rougher guys, you were always so polite. And never let anyone get unruly in the bar."

He nodded. "I wanted to make sure everyone stayed in line."

"Nice of you to do that for a waitress," she said.

"Not a waitress. You."

"But why?" she asked. "You want me to believe you just walked in and it was love at first sight?"

He pressed his lips into a line and considered how to explain it without his bear in the equation. "You're beautiful and strong. You're kind and didn't act afraid of me because of my size. I was always just trying to get up the courage to speak to you."

She put a hand to her head and let out a shaky laugh. "I can't believe this. I couldn't get up the courage to talk to you either. Something about you just drew me in."

He pulled her onto his lap, cradling her against him, feeling secure now that she was safe and in his arms. "I'm glad it was mutual." At least the attraction. He knew her love for him wouldn't be instant like his was for her, but it could grow in time, as it did for humans.

She reached up and ran a hand along his five o'clock shadow, scratching the stubble there that had sprung up in only one day. Zeus blamed his bear.

"So what should we do next?" she asked. She moved a hand down over his button again, teasing him, and Zeus groaned at the temptation but pulled back, shaking his head.

"Not tonight," he said. "We need to rest. And I can't believe I'm saying this, but I want to take it slow with you."

"It's a little late for that," she said, giggling.

"All right, then," he said. "Let's do something slow and romantic tonight. What do couples usually do on dates?"

"Well, they usually go out, but we can't."

"Okay," he said. "How about I take you to a movie, then?"

She gave him a puzzled look. "Um, we can't go out."

"Right, but Ares's home theater is pretty kick ass. We can watch one of those chick flicks women like so much."

She shook her head. "Nah, I'm more of a horror movie fan."

His eyebrows shot up. "Really?"

She nodded. "Come on. I'll help you pick a really good one. And don't worry. If you get scared, I'll comfort you." She laughed and helped him up.

"All right," he said, leading the way to the basement. "As long as you stay here with me and protect me," he teased.

She laughed, and he couldn't resist swatting her on the butt as she went down the stairs ahead of him.

A horror movie would be perfect. Carly would be disappointed though, because nothing in the movies could ever scare Zeus. Only one thing in the world could, and that was her being in danger. And Zeus would never let that happen.

They settled into the comfy recliners and he put an arm up for her to snuggle under, and they picked out a new zombie movie that Carly hadn't seen.

With his phone close so he'd hear any alarm, Zeus allowed himself to relax with his mate.

CHAPTER 10

When the movie ended, Carly was too comfortable cuddling with Zeus and didn't want to move. But it was late, and Zeus said he wanted to call Ares and check up on how things were going, so he walked her up to a bedroom across from his, made sure she was comfortable, and then went back to his room.

She hugged a pillow and lay back on the bed. The curtains were closed, but there wouldn't be any beautiful view outside anyway. Not from Ares's concrete fortress.

Still, she was having fun here, as long as it was with Zeus. She still had warm fuzzies from what he'd said about coming to the bar just to see her. It wasn't any promise of a future, but it meant he'd thought of her before. Like she'd thought of him. That he'd been interested even before they'd been thrown together in this Devils situation.

She still didn't know what the future held exactly, but she liked the way it was headed.

She liked the way Zeus looked at her, with that intense, possessive gaze.

Her old boyfriend hadn't even been willing to face debt for her, yet this man had faced gunfire.

She heard Zeus finish his call and opened her door to find him pacing the hall. His square, masculine features were tensed slightly, as if he were thinking something over.

"Is everything okay?" she asked.

He looked so handsome in a flannel shirt that outlined his broad shoulders and perfectly cut pecs. The sleeves were rolled up, baring muscular arms that she longed to put her hands all over. And his abs…

Her mouth watered.

She wanted this man like she'd never wanted anyone, and it seemed like a hunger that would never cease.

But he'd already said no for tonight.

His eyes met hers as he tucked the phone away in his pants.

"Everything's fine," he said. "They're searching the woods, just like we want them to. They can search for days up there. It's dark and easy to get lost in."

She nodded. But somehow she knew she'd never get lost up there with Zeus. She could see it being a home for them.

Home. That was an odd word. She'd wanted to stay in Bearstone Village and pay her debts, but she'd never thought of this place as home. Now she was starting to think of Zeus as home. But was she just a silly girl getting carried away by the first man to be truly good to her?

Was Zeus planning for this to end when she wasn't in danger any longer? She didn't think so, but she'd been abandoned before, and she hadn't seen that coming either.

Still, she wouldn't think the worst about Zeus when he'd been nothing but kind to her.

She went to him and curled her arms around his waist. Every moment with him was precious, and with the danger facing them, who knew what would happen in the next hours or days? Carly wanted to live life to the fullest, wanted to take everything Zeus had to offer while things were still good.

And her body ached to feel him again.

"Zeus?" she asked. "Are you sure we can't do anything tonight?" Her hand found his tight butt and gave a squeeze, and he groaned as he rested his lips on her hair in a soft kiss.

"I don't know," he said. "It's been a long day. I know you're tired. We both need our rest for tomorrow."

"Just a little?" she asked, looking up at him with pleading eyes. Anything would do, and she could see he wanted her as much as she wanted him. A little drowsiness would be worth it.

"All right," he said, a gleam in his eyes as he hoisted her in his arms. "Just a little."

She tried to get down. "It's okay. Don't carry me. You're still—"

"It'll be a cold day in hell when I can't carry my woman to bed to please her," Zeus growled, kicking open the door to his room and laying her on the massive bed. He came over her and nuzzled her neck. "Now, how about that little something you asked for?"

She sighed against him. She couldn't help but trust Zeus. Something inside her just responded to him. Felt right with him. Never wanted to leave him.

Zeus placed a soft kiss on Carly's neck, sending a tiny shock of pleasure through her before she could respond. She loved the feel of his huge, hard body against her softness. Loved the way he gave her everything, made her feel special and wonderful all at the same time.

Holding her close, he moved up to take her lips in a long, hard kiss that was as strong as it was sweet. She opened her mouth instantly, and he came inside, each stroke more passionate and precise than the last. Just the way his tongue roved inside her mouth blew her mind, making her want more and more.

He left her mouth, leaving Carly breathless and euphoric, and ran his fingers along the exposed skin at the bottom of her shirt. He pushed the hem up slightly and kissed along the waistband of her pants, then over her soft belly, coming to her belly button. He kissed it once, then ran his tongue along the edge. At first, the sensation was arousing and ticklish, but the more he did it, the more she relaxed into a steadily building pleasure.

Zeus licked inside her belly button, and it sent another shock of pleasure down her spine. He looked up at her with his deep-blue eyes, dark and intoxicating, and just the sight of his aroused gaze turned her on further.

Carly moved to take off her shirt, but Zeus stopped her, holding both her hands in his. To her surprise, he took each of them and examined them closely, rubbing his thumbs along her knuckles. He isolated one finger on her right hand and drew it to his mouth, kissing it first, then bringing his lips around it and sucking on it.

At first, Carly was confused, but the second his lips touched her, her skin lit on fire where he touched it and lightning trailed all the way from her finger down to her toes. When he kissed between her knuckles at the base of her index and middle finger, even more pleasure shot through her, drawing a sigh from her lips.

"How are you doing that?" Carly asked, surprised.

"It's you. Your beauty. You're so perfect everywhere, Carly. I'm just showing you how much," Zeus said, then took her other hand to his mouth and gave the same treatment.

She'd never known she could feel so much in the different parts of her body. No man had ever taken the time to find out. And now, having this amazing, gentle, powerful man exploring every inch of her, she could barely believe it was happening.

He kissed up her hands and over her arms, each sensitive inch lighting up at his touch.

Already, she was so turned on, so pent up; she wasn't sure how much longer she could wait for the main event.

Carly reached out for Zeus's pants and tried to unbutton them, but he stopped her, holding her hands in his.

"Not that. Not tonight," he said.

Carly folded her arms and pouted, making Zeus smile.

"I promise to make it up to you," he said, pulling off her pants in one swift, smooth motion. She was wearing a pair of soft, pink panties with a lacy fringe, and Zeus ran his hands up the length of her thighs, coming painfully close to the center of her hips before coming back down. He was torturing her with every touch. And she loved it.

First he kissed the tops of her feet, then licked a long trail up the inside of one leg, working past the knee and all the way inside her thigh. He stopped right as he reached the edge of her underwear and then came up the other leg and did the same. Every time he came nearer, nearer to where she wanted him most. Even the smallest touch was like a blazing fire, a burning heat that could only be quenched by release, which he held the key to.

After that, he ran his fingers right across the top of her underwear, playing with it and passing his fingers under it ever so slightly. As he did that, he licked along the same edge, coming so close yet feeling like a million miles from exactly where her body screamed for him to touch.

All of the foreplay was so hot, so thoroughly sensual. But she couldn't hold on much longer. It was driving her mad with lust, and every nerve in Carly's body was tensed, coiled, waiting to explode.

As if he could hear her thoughts, Zeus held both her hips with his huge hands and came down and placed one long, hard kiss at her center. Even through her panties, the perfect, insanely hot pressure drove her over the edge of desire. Her entire body shuddered, the built tension releasing through wave after wave of pleasure coursing through every nerve and vein. Carly screamed out Zeus's name as he came over her and held her in his arms. She dug her nails into his back, wanting to avoid touching anywhere near his wound but unable to form any other cogent thoughts, and rode out the rapid succession of sweeping release coming through her.

Before Carly had even fully relaxed, Zeus hooked a finger on each side of her panties and gave her a wicked look. Carly was still wearing the T-shirt she'd put on, and normally, she would have expected both of them to have more clothes off before going to that. But for some reason, still being partially clothed and Zeus still having his shirt and jeans on felt hot and naughty. Like there wasn't time for disrobing, just pleasure. The pleasure he wanted to give her and the lust she had for him that he alone could satisfy.

With a smooth motion, her panties were gone, leaving her bared, and Zeus spread Carly's legs, filling her with thrilling anticipation.

No man had ever given her this much pleasure. Ever.

That thought was interrupted as he placed several soft kisses at the apex of her thighs, lightly brushing her with his lips. Every touch was lightning on her skin, more intense now that she had come once already. He extended a finger and ran it once, slowly, against her clit, and her body arched off the bed from the incredible pleasure.

Zeus slipped a finger inside her, feeling her wetness, stroking gently and hooking upward to touch her most sensitive spot. It wasn't the same as having him inside, but it still felt amazing.

"You're so wet, so ready for me," Zeus said, pulling out his finger and licking it, looking pleased.

The sight was so hot. In the air, she could pick up what must have been his scent again, masculine and musky. Everything he did drove her further and further into the throes of unimaginable pleasure.

He dipped in his finger again and brought his other hand to her clit, holding his finger directly over it, but not moving. She could feel the intensity of the pleasure, anticipated it. Every fiber of her being wanted it, wanted him.

"You like that, don't you?" Zeus said, his voice low and commanding.

Her body felt suspended, waiting and wanting him to keep moving. It was as if he held her entire body in his control with only two fingers.

"I'm the only man that turns you on like this," he said possessively. Both a question and a statement.

"Don't stop," she pleaded.

"Say it," he commanded her.

"You're the only one," she responded hoarsely. Every nerve was waiting for him.

"The only one who…" he said, his intense blue eyes watching her intently, heated and dark in the low light.

"The only one who turns me on like this."

"Damn straight," Zeus said as he stroked inside and on her clit at the same time, both fingers moving right across the pinnacles of her personal pleasure in one smooth motion.

Her entire body came apart again, grasping at the headboard, the sheets, anywhere she could hold as she orgasmed. Her legs clenched around Zeus's hand, and she saw him give her a heated, satisfied smile that owned her.

Carly didn't know how long they had together. She only hoped it would be forever. Because even forever would never be long enough to fully receive the amount of pleasure he alone gave her.

She came down from the orgasm, feeling even better than after the first, and stretched out over the bed.

"Zeus, that was amazing. Thank you," she said. Her entire body hummed with satisfaction.

"You're not done. Not yet," Zeus said assertively.

Carly looked up at him wide-eyed as he came over her and gave a long, deliciously pleasurable lick over her clit. She moaned loudly at the sensation and closed her eyes, overcome by the shockingly good feeling it gave her.

This man was entirely overwhelming in every way.

And she loved it.

Zeus held her thighs with his hands, anchoring her as he stroked her again and again with his tongue, slowly and thoroughly. Her body moved in time with him, pushing against his tongue to increase the intensity even further. The rhythm was ecstasy, driving her quickly to one more release.

Carly felt completely engulfed in the experience. The sight of Zeus's head below her, intensely focused on her. His smell filling the air. The touch of his hands holding her. The sound of her hurried breathing, trying to hold back the inevitable. So much.

Zeus gave one last stroke, and Carly felt herself careen past the boundaries of the pleasure building in her, sending her into a euphoric release stronger than any other. This time, he came over her and held her tightly to him, surrounding her and protecting her as she melted in his arms and rode out the incredible release.

If this was a fantasy, she never wanted it to end.

Once her body had relaxed, feeling fully satiated and unable to take any more, Zeus pulled the sheets over them and came behind her, spooning her. He wrapped both arms around her, making her feel so safe, and Carly gave out a long, satisfied sigh.

"That was incredible," she said. "Now you."

He shook his head. "Not tonight."

"But… I can't just… take everything." Disappointment surged through her, but she knew he had his reasons. Still, she wanted to see her big man lost in the throes of pleasure, growling her name as he pumped inside her.

"You can and you will," he said. "I love giving you pleasure. But that's all I can do. At least for tonight."

"All right," she said, snuggling into him as the feel of her afterglow gushed through her, uninterrupted this time. "But you better make it up to me next time."

He kissed the top of her head. "It's a promise."

They held each other until they relaxed, and Carly turned to Zeus, a question in her eyes. "Can I sleep in here tonight?"

He growled and pulled her against his chest. "I wouldn't have it any other way. I want you right here where I can protect you. Pleasure you."

She laughed at his possessiveness. "All right. Then here is where I'll stay."

She was rewarded with a long, deep kiss that blanketed her with peace, a full feeling of well-being, and as she snuggled into a comfortable position beside him, she knew this was exactly where she belonged.

CHAPTER 11

The next morning, Zeus looked down at his mate in his arms and felt a surge of protectiveness flow through him.

She was beautiful. More than beautiful, she was incredible. Her silky brown hair was splayed over his pillow and her soft body rested in his arms. Her lashes rested on her cheeks as she let out quiet, peaceful snores. He wanted to just stay there with her, watching her, imagining he'd already told her and they were bound together forever, but he had other things to do.

It had been torture to wait, to hold back and not claim her. His bear had known it was so close; it would have been so easy to just take her right there. He knew if he lost control, if he let himself go inside her, his animal would take over, and he couldn't let that happen yet. Perhaps he was a coward, but he just wasn't ready to go over all of that with Carly yet. They had time, right?

Just as the thought passed through his mind, the door to the house opened and slammed closed, and he heard Ares's heavy footsteps in the living room, smelled Ares's scent. He crept quietly out of bed, making sure she was still sleeping soundly, and walked out of the bedroom and down the hallway, still wearing his rumpled clothes from yesterday.

Ares was sitting at the counter, looking tired, faint dark circles under his brilliant green eyes. He looked up at Zeus with a wry grin and raised a mug in toast. "To long nights in the woods with criminals."

Zeus frowned and joined him at the counter. "What happened?"

"They roped me into helping," he said. "It would have looked bad if your best friend wasn't up there looking for you too. They aren't sure where to look now that the woods seem to be clear, but my guess is they'll regroup and try to come here soon."

Zeus nodded. He got up and poured himself a cup of coffee and sipped it as he sat next to Ares. Ares sniffed the air and looked at his friend suspiciously.

"What?" Zeus asked, avoiding his gaze.

"You smell different," Ares said, scenting the air and then laughing and pushing his hair off his forehead. "Nice job."

Zeus growled. "I don't know what you're talking about."

"Yeah, you do," Ares said, grinning and sitting up a little straighter. "Did you claim her?"

"No," Zeus snapped. "You know it wouldn't be right. Not with all the things I can't tell her yet."

Ares sighed. "Look, man, you know I respect you. But I think you're going about this thing with Carly the wrong way. You're going to give her the wrong idea."

"What do you mean?" Zeus asked.

"You know, doing this kind of thing with a woman, you need to be clear with her on what the end game is. Otherwise, it's going to be real awkward when this whole thing is over."

"What do you mean?" he asked.

"You know, when the Devils are handled and you two don't have an excuse to live together anymore," Ares said, waving a hand. "A woman like that, she's gonna want some regular commitment, to start dating like an average couple, and you know that's not how it works for men like us. We don't do normal," Ares said.

Zeus nodded. His bear didn't want normal. Didn't want to let Carly go back to her apartment and her job and let him show up now and then to take her on dates. He wanted to propose to her now, tell her everything about his bear and how much he wanted her, and take her back to his cabin in the woods to live happily ever after.

But if he told her before this was all over, she might end up running or not want him to keep protecting her, knowing he'd been pursuing her from the start. Maybe she'd think he was a stalker or crazy. And all of those things could lead to her leaving his side and not allowing him to protect her.

The thought of Carly captured by the mob, taken from him forever, beaten or bruised or worse, filled his mind and made a low growl rumble from his chest.

"Hey, don't get mad at me for saying what has to be done," Ares said, misunderstanding the direction of Zeus's anger. "I mean, what happens if you don't tell her?" Ares raised an eyebrow at him. "You just take her back to your cabin and go along with this make-believe game and keep dating her? Meanwhile, she goes along with it in ignorance, not knowing it isn't what you want at all?"

"You don't understand," Zeus said. "I'm going to tell her. I just think it's best to wait until this thing with the Devils is over and I don't need her to stay." Then the only thing at risk if she ran would be his own heart and hopes. And he could handle that, as long as he knew she was safe.

Ares shook his head. "I still think you're playing with fire, my friend. And I think you're underestimating Carly's ability to handle the truth. She's a big girl. But I guess you're right. We have other shit to deal with. The Devils are probably regrouping as we speak. They were up all night and are probably still recovering from the bear attack, but they'll be back soon. And they'll want Carly."

"Right," Zeus said. And he'd never let them take her. He and Ares would just have to put their heads together and hurry and solve the Devils issue once and for all so he could finally take his mate aside and tell her just what she meant to him.

But in the meantime, his bear's need to reveal itself would have to take a backseat to her safety.

* * *

Carly stayed pressed against her closed door, heart silently breaking at what she'd heard.

She hadn't meant to eavesdrop. She'd just wanted to sneak out and surprise Zeus with a hug and kiss while he was eating his breakfast.

Last night had been wonderful, another step in what she thought was a promising relationship. Even though Zeus had never said anything explicitly, she'd always felt a sort of commitment from him. And he didn't seem like the type of man who would say sweet things to a woman and then just walk away.

But Carly had been abandoned before. She knew how quickly a man could go from whispering sweet nothings in the dark to taking the next ride out of town, leaving her to pick up the broken pieces.

But she'd tried not to think about it with Zeus, tried to be open to something new and trust he wouldn't hurt her.

Perhaps it was all her fault for getting her hopes up again. For seeing forever in a man's eyes when he only saw today.

But his conversation with Ares had been more than clear. He'd admitted to Ares he couldn't just go on dating normally after this was over, that men like that didn't do "normal."

He meant military men, she supposed. Men who fought and lived a rough life alone. It made sense. Zeus had lived solitary in those woods for so long.

What made her think he would want company now?

And Ares had called him on the fact that if they kept going as they were, they'd be living a lie. That Zeus would be continuing things with her just because he was afraid to cut them off. The picture Ares had painted of an ignorant life with Zeus at his cabin was Carly's worst nightmare.

She wasn't angry with Ares, though. Someone had to say something. At least now she knew what she'd never had the courage to ask Zeus. Where this was going. Apparently, it was going nowhere, and he didn't want to tell her that until he had to.

Right now, he could have his cake and eat it too. Keep her there trusting him, knowing she didn't have a choice with the Red Devils hunting her, and then tell her at the end, when things would be at a natural close.

Why had she assumed when he'd said he'd always been interested that it meant he wanted a long-term commitment? Why did she keep thinking men would want to settle down and make a home when it was clear there was only one thing they wanted?

Hurt broke through her. The hurt of her ex leaving her with all their debts, which she hadn't even fully processed. The hurt of Zeus, too afraid to tell her he wasn't looking to date her normally after all this was over. The hurt of being unwanted once again.

Well, that wasn't entirely true. Zeus definitely wanted her. She'd seen it in his eyes, in the way he made love to her. For all she knew, when it was over, he'd propose some arrangement where they still got hot and heavy at times but never settled into anything "normal" like a couple would.

After all, men like him didn't, apparently.

She folded her arms and let the tears stream down her cheeks, trying to gather strength inside her to make her next move. Despite what Zeus thought, she wasn't an idiot. She wasn't going to just run out and get captured just because she was angry that things with Zeus weren't what she thought.

For all she knew, that was all he was capable of. Maybe he cared but just couldn't do normal relationships.

Maybe that's why it felt like he was holding out last night. He hadn't wanted to have sex, had been content to just pleasure her. And it had been hot, if incomplete somehow.

But perhaps that's why he was holding back. He was probably realizing just how much she was falling in love with him and was trying to let her down easy while still giving her what he thought she wanted.

But she didn't want Zeus living a lie for her. Didn't want him spending even another moment lying to her to spare her feelings.

If he knew he didn't want anything when this was over, then she didn't either. She'd live. She'd go back to the bar, work off her debt, and try not to think of the sexy man in the mountains who'd blown her world apart in all the right ways. And all the wrong ones.

She swiped tears off her cheeks as she heard footsteps in the hall. Panic swept through her. She wasn't ready to face him. She walked away from the door and stood with her back to the window, as far from him as possible. When the door slowly opened, she brushed her hair back behind her ears and tried to look calm, as if nothing were bothering her.

She didn't need to make things more awkward for him.

When Zeus walked in, looking painfully handsome in a loose tee and fitted jeans, his hair freshly combed through with his fingers, his blue eyes looking bright and aware, she almost felt herself falling for him again. She'd never stop wanting him, no matter who he thought he was or how unsuitable he was for commitment.

He saw her face and his expression dropped. She

should have known she couldn't hide her feelings for him. For better or worse, she just wasn't someone who could play games.

She took a step forward, unsure what to say, then heard a scratching noise above them like something was on the roof. A second later, the ground trembled as something huge dropped down behind her. The window shattered, and she felt something grab her by the back of her shirt and haul her out of the cabin and onto the ground. She saw Zeus running toward her but was quickly grabbed again by the collar and thrown onto the back of a huge animal as it ran for the gate surrounding the home.

She saw Zeus climbing out of the window, yelling for Ares, as the bear scaled the gate and then dropped on the other side, letting her roll off its back just as men came out of the woods and grabbed her by the arms.

She screamed for Zeus as they forced her into an old Jeep and took off.

CHAPTER 12

Zeus couldn't believe it. This whole time, they'd had a bear hiding out on their damn roof. It could climbed up there before Ares had even turned on the perimeter alarm, long before Zeus and Ares had been forced to come back here after the attack at the cabin.

It was a great way to hide out without tripping any cameras, and since neither Zeus nor Ares had known the Devils had a bear shifter in their mix that could scale a roof like that, they'd never have guessed this could happen.

But Zeus didn't have time to berate himself for all the things he didn't plan for. He had to get Carly back and run the Red Devils out of town for good so this could never happen again.

He ran across the courtyard after the bear who'd taken Carly, transforming as he went. With a roar, he bounded over the gate just in time to see a Jeep taking off into the forest. He roared again when he saw a bear running behind it, nearly out of sight.

He'd follow that. And just hope Ares knew how and when to show up for support. He didn't have time for fancy plans or military tactics. Right now he was just a rabid bear chasing the men who had taken his mate. And he was going to kill every last fucking one of them.

He tracked them through the forest, to the main part of town, and out of town, where the paved roads turned to dirt roads. He could see what must be their compound in the distance. Just outside it was the El Diablo bar, the notorious hangout for the Red Devils and their cronies. Beyond that lay a small warehouse surrounded by a sheet metal fence. The fence was closed, and in front of it stood two men, both holding shotguns.

Zeus's bear didn't need weapons or the upper hand. All he needed was four paws, a giant mouth lined with teeth, a thick hide that only the heaviest of bullets could pierce, and a burning rage that would not be quenched until his mate was safe.

Throwing precaution to the wind, Zeus charged up the hill. At first, the two men looked to each other, bewildered at the sight of a gigantic bear running toward them. But bewilderment turned quickly to fear, and both fumbled with the lock of the gate, trying to get inside before he could reach them.

But it was too late. With one swipe, both men went flying to the side. Then Zeus swung his great paw at the fence, ripping into the sheet metal that was little more than paper to his bear. A section of fence toppled to the ground in a cloud of dust, and Zeus ran inside the small compound.

It was little more than a large garage connected to an old office that had probably been the home of a repair shop for semi trucks or something like that long ago. Now, it was the hideout for the Red Devils. And even though yesterday's fight had probably cut heavily into their numbers, he knew they were inside, waiting for him. He could scent them, each and every one, with his bear's heightened sense of smell.

He could also scent his mate, her fear. It filled his bear with rage.

The garage had two heavy steel doors that were swung wide open, inviting him in. It was a trap; he knew one when he saw it. But he didn't care. If it was the only way to save his mate, he'd face fire and death for her.

Zeus approached the garage but saw no one. He stepped inside, could feel eyes watching him, smell just how close they were by their filthy stench.

A door opened that led onto a high catwalk some twenty feet above the ground that ran around the edges of the interior. In stepped several armed thugs and a large man dressed in a worn vest and a red bandana bearing the Devils's insignia. He was around the same age as Zeus, but his face was craggy and hardened, with dark, shaggy hair hanging around it.

The bear shifter. Zeus would bet his life on it.

Dragging behind him, held by one hand, was Carly. She looked terrified, and the sight of Zeus's bear in the center of the room didn't seem to bring her any additional peace. Right now, he hated that she didn't know who he was, that he was here for her.

"So the bear returns for second helpings. Not today," the man holding Carly called to Zeus, mocking him. From the obvious looks of it, he was the leader, which made sense. Even a weak bear shifter was several times stronger than the hardest of humans.

As much as Zeus wanted to call the bear shifter

out with human words, it was forbidden to speak in shifter form around humans unless they were your mate. So instead of speaking, he let out a long roar that reverberated off the concrete and metal walls of the garage, filling the room. Some of the men cowered, looking shaken.

"I don't know who you or your friends are, and I don't care," the leader said. "This town is mine, and just as soon as we take care of the little lady here," he said, glaring down at Carly momentarily, "then nobody will be able to stop us." He paused, then raised his hand and brought it down in a swift motion. "Attack!"

The men in the room fired upon him, and more started pouring in from a small entrance on the other side. Behind him, the large steel door swung closed, barring his escape.

Just as Zeus had suspected, it was a trap. And this time, the Devils were much better prepared to fight a bear. Instead of pistols, they were using military-grade weaponry, probably the kind of weapons they dealt illegally to criminals all around this region.

But Zeus kept his cool. His bear knew what to do. Moving on instinct, he ducked behind a row of shelves and toolboxes, out of the line of fire. He then made for the entrance at the side where men were coming in, and charged a small Jeep parked at the corner of the garage, ramming it forward with a slam into the door, blocking the entrance.

The few men that had been able to come in on the first floor panicked, and he swiped at them, sending them into walls and crashing through windows.

But above him, the men on the raised second and third story walkways had repositioned and begun to fire on him. Even with their improper training, Zeus could feel the hail of bullets falling around him, several of them hitting him in the side.

Even with his thick hide and regenerative powers, that kind of firepower was more than he could handle. He ran and ducked behind a truck parked near the back, hoping to buy time.

Zeus was trapped. If he tried to move into the open, they'd have a clear shot at him. With his bear strength, he could easily knock out the support columns of the building and bring it down, but that would be far too dangerous for Carly. And with the main doors closed, there was no way out.

Besides, retreat was never an option anyway.

Zeus huffed and readied to charge at the men coming down onto the first floor just ahead of him, when his bear hearing picked up a sound in the distance, high-pitched and whirring, fast approaching their direction.

In an instant, the heavy steel doors exploded in an inferno of fire and metal, sending the men who were standing in the center of the garage flying backward from the force of it. Even behind the truck, Zeus felt the impact.

From years of combat, he knew what had hit the doors just now.

A rocket launcher.

As the flames cleared in a cloud of gray smoke, Zeus made out a large, black truck zooming up the hill toward them. It stopped abruptly at the entrance to the garage in a cloud of dust that intermingled with the lingering smoke, and Zeus saw Ares jump out of the cab, a gun in both hands and several more strapped on slings around his back.

But before Ares could even open fire, Zeus heard a loud pop in the distance. Then a millisecond later, he watched as one of the thugs on a raised platform went limp and careened over the railing. It was the sound of a sniper rifle, probably several hundred meters off in the distance.

Ares had brought Hades to the fight as well.

"Yeah, fuckers, you picked the wrong town to mess with," Ares called out as he fired on the men inside, many of them still dazed by the explosion. With incredible speed and accuracy, Ares emptied an entire magazine of ammunition, dropped the gun without reloading it, and pulled another from his back.

Zeus might have been their commander, but Ares was the pride of the battalion as far as marksmanship and weapons-handling was concerned. He'd been the one to fire the rocket launcher earlier, probably getting in the truck again right after.

With the goons inside taking cover behind crates and toolboxes and whatever they could use to shield themselves from the onslaught of fire, Zeus charged forward and tore through the unsuspecting thugs. In no time at all, they were retreating fully, jumping through windows and crawling for exits as fast as they could.

Outside, Zeus could hear the sound of motorcycles starting and, soon after, saw men driving away from the garage and heading for the highway that led out of town.

"You find Carly. I'll call Hades and get his help chasing stragglers. We'll make sure they get the going away party they deserve," Ares said, tossing his guns into the back of the pickup and hopping in, making down the road after the fleeing motorcycles.

Zeus nodded and continued to run, knowing the Devils would be out of his way for good, but there was still one man here not ready to stand down, and he still held Zeus's mate.

"Not a step farther, bear. I know what you're here for," Zeus heard the leader call above him, his voice clear in the large garage.

Zeus stopped and looked up to see them both standing on the raised metal walkway. Carly was held tightly by the bear shifter, one arm wrapped around her and the other holding a gun pointed at her.

There was only one man left between him and his mate.

With the fight over, the room was empty, with only the sound of far-off engines and a few lingering flames crackling and slowly dying out to be heard.

"You've taken everything from me. My men, my resources. Everything I've worked to build for over ten years," he said, sounding angry and desperate. "So I'm going to take the one thing I know you care about more than anything else in the whole world." When the man finished, he turned from Zeus to Carly, looking at her with an evil smile.

He was going to claim Carly before Zeus could. Zeus roared in anger at the man.

"Not so fast, bear. Make one move and I'll kill

the girl. I want you to change back so you don't get any funny ideas about trying to save her," the man yelled down at him.

Zeus quieted the raging bear inside him and focused. If he was going to get Carly out of this, it was going to take planning and precision, not brawn.

It took all of his mental fortitude to shift out of his bear and back into his human form, the bear inside still raging and roaring for the man's blood. And as he shifted, Zeus could see shock and bewilderment in Carly's eyes.

He hadn't been planning to tell her this way. But he had no choice. This was his only chance to save her.

"That's more like it," the leader said with a sneer. "It's too bad, really. When we picked her up off the street earlier, I could scent you on her. The same scent I picked up in the mountains when we were looking for you. You came so close to having her, didn't you?" he mocked, looking smug and running a finger down the side of Carly's face. She winced and cringed at the man's touch but kept her eyes on Zeus.

Despite all of this, she still trusted him.

For a split second, the man's finger left the trigger of the gun as he ominously touched Carly's cheek, seemingly pleased with himself. Zeus sprang into action, more than a decade of hardened military experience and supernatural shifter reflexes working as one.

Everything happened in slow motion. He reached for a nearby rifle that had been left on the floor by a fleeing thug, and as he brought the gun to his shoulder, he chambered a round with a swift flick. Above him, he could see the man reacting and pointing the gun down at him. But no matter how fast he was, Zeus was faster. With trained precision and perfect accuracy, he glanced down the sights, took aim, and fired, putting a bullet right through the shifter's head.

The lone sound of the shot echoed through the room, and a second later, the leader's grip on Carly slackened for a moment. Then the gun dropped from his hand and he slumped over to the side. Carly fell to her knees, away from the dead body, and Zeus started for the stairs that led up to his mate.

But out of nowhere, Zeus heard the rusted metal grating that comprised the walkway groan and crack. A moment later, it gave way, dropping out from beneath Carly and sending her careening over the edge, screaming.

In an instant, Zeus was there beneath her. She fell

into his arms with a thud, and for a moment, she just looked at him, eyes wide with confusion.

There was a lot to figure out between them. But for now, she was safe. That was all that mattered.

CHAPTER 13

He picked her up in his arms and carried her out of the compound and into the brush where it was a little more private. He sat down on a large, overturned log with her in his lap, and she let out a long breath as she stared up wide-eyed at his face.

"I'm sorry," he said. "I wanted to tell you, I was just waiting for the right time."

She nodded slowly, still stiff with shock. Whether it was from finding out he could shift into a bear or because she'd narrowly escaped a terrible fate at the hands of the Red Devils, he didn't know.

"Thank you for rescuing me," she said, taking her hands with his and pressing them to her face. "You're always rescuing me."

"Of course," he said, brushing hair off her face. "I'll always rescue you. Whenever you need it."

She blinked and dropped his hands. "Right, I guess I don't need it anymore." She pushed against him, presumably trying to get out of his lap and stand.

What was this? Was this where she left him, because she couldn't handle what he was?

He couldn't let her.

He reached out and grabbed her hand, pulling her back in against him. "Don't go," he said, holding her close as if he could keep her there by sheer force.

"What?" she said, looking up at him. "I mean, I heard you and Ares talking this morning. About, you know, ending it when this was over."

His brow crinkled in confusion. "I didn't say anything like that. What are you talking about?"

She looked stunned, then bit her lip in embarrassment. "I heard you two talking. Ares said you needed to tell me that men like you, men in the military, can't do normal."

"Right," Zeus said, exhaling in relief at the misunderstanding. "But not because of the military, but because we are bears. I couldn't just slip into a life with you without telling you who I was. That's all he meant." He realized how it must have sounded to someone who didn't know about shifters. "Damn it, I'm sorry. I've messed everything up. But I swear I was only trying to protect you."

She sighed in relief and relaxed against him, her entire body going limp. "You've definitely protected me," she said weakly. "But I think you better tell me the rest right now. Because my heart can't take any more secrets or misunderstandings."

"Okay," he said. "First off, Carly, you mean everything to me."

"How can that be?" she asked. "You barely know me."

"My bear knew from the moment he saw you. He's my heart, deep inside me. My instinct, my strength. And he knew you were perfect for me, even if I was so taken off guard that I didn't know what to do about it."

She just listened, still looking dazed.

The forest was quiet around them, the perfect place for him to tell her everything. He only wished they hadn't had to go through the past few hours first.

"I'm sorry you got caught up in all of this, but I'm not sorry it gave me a chance to spend time with you. After the past couple days together, the man in me is positive of what the bear in me knew from the start." He took her hand and tenderly kissed the top of it. "You're it for me, Carly. You're this lonely bear's home."

She was too touched to say anything, just watched him as he continued to kiss her hand, gently, over each knuckle. Then he sat back to talk again.

"When I got out of the military, I just wanted somewhere quiet. Ares convinced me to come back here to his hometown, and the moment I saw the beautiful woods, I knew I'd found a home." He looked at the mountains rising up all around them. "I've found a lot of healing here, but I never knew I would find my mate."

He brushed his thumb over her cheek and took her mouth in a deep kiss, trying to tell her with more than words just how he felt about her. She kissed him back, tongue entwining with his as the world seemed to freeze around them.

Then she pulled back and looked at him breathlessly. "So what does being a mate even mean?"

He stroked a hand over her back soothingly. "It means something like marriage, but stronger. It means I'm yours forever, and you're mine, once we complete the ceremony and become mates."

"Mates," she said. "I like the sound of that. But

Ares wasn't kidding. None of this is normal. When I saw you turn from bear to human, I nearly had a heart attack."

"I'm sorry," he said. "I should have told you sooner, but I didn't want you to run."

"I wouldn't have run," she said. "I care about you too much. I guess I'm still having a hard time letting it all sink in. I mean, I get that your bear wants me, but why do you want me?"

He nuzzled into her hair. "I love your curves, the way your nose wrinkles when you smile. I love making love to you, the way your beautiful body responds to my hands. I love how you trust me, how you've always trusted me, even when everyone else treated me like a scary stranger. I love your kindness and open heart."

She let out a long breath but stayed silent in his arms, resting her hand against his bare skin.

"From the moment you got on my bike, you've been giving this soldier bear peace he's never known or ever thought to have. Please say you'll stay with me, Carly. We don't have to live in the mountains if you'd rather come down to the town. We don't even have to stay in Bearstone Village. As long as you say you'll stay with me forever, anywhere we go will be home."

She laughed. "You silly bear. Of course we'll stay in the mountains."

"Then it's a yes?"

"Yes," she said. "I've never been happier than when I'm with you. I can't imagine anything else. But what is the mating ceremony you talked about? Is it complicated?"

"Not really," he said. "And the first part, I know you'll love. Sex, with nothing between us."

"Sounds good to me," she said eagerly.

He laughed. "The second part is simply approving and accepting my bear."

"How do I do that?"

"You kiss him," he said.

She nodded seriously. "I can do that. Now that I know he's just part of you, another side of you, it all makes sense. Your bear is as badass as you are."

"Thanks," he said, standing with her in his arms. "Now we just have to wait for Ares to get back."

"And then back to your place?"

"Back to my place," he agreed. "I'm not waiting another second to make you mine."

"Well, I'd sort of like a bath and a meal, if that's okay with you."

"All right," he said. "But you drive a hard bargain."

Just then, the rumble of Ares's truck reached their ears and they saw it turn up the road to the compound. Zeus set her down beside him and walked forward to meet his friend.

Ares grinned as he got out and handed Zeus a bag filled with clothing. As Zeus dressed, Ares let out a whistle in Carly's direction. "So I guess things are okay now? Phew, you guys scared me for a bit there."

Zeus nodded in relief and then looked around them. "Where's Hades?"

Ares shrugged. "You know Hades. He's always happy to support when you need him, but prefers to stay out of sight and disappear as needed."

Zeus pulled the shirt over his head and slid the cargo pants over his legs. "Thanks for calling him in. And coming to support."

"Always, boss."

"If you ever need me to return the favor…"

Ares grinned. "Alpha squadron forever."

"Forever," Zeus agreed.

Ares scratched his head as Zeus got in the back of the cab with Carly, lifting her onto his lap possessively. "Damn, now I just gotta find me one of these."

"What?" Carly asked.

"A cute little mate to cuddle," Ares said, getting

into the driver's seat and starting the engine.

"Like anyone would want to cuddle your gun-crazy ass," Zeus said, drawing a laugh from Ares.

"Hey, if it could happen to your reclusive butt, it could happen for anyone," he said.

"Even Hades?" Zeus joked.

"Um, yeah. I don't know about that one." Ares laughed. "Anyway, he's gotta wait his turn. I'm taking the next one."

"Right now, all you're doing is taking us home," Zeus grumbled as Ares pulled onto the driveway.

"Fine, fine," Ares said, guiding the truck over the bumpy, uneven dirt in the direction of Zeus's cabin. "I get it. The big, bad bear wants to go home and claim his mate."

Damn straight. Zeus wouldn't be happy until Carly was officially his.

CHAPTER 14

When they got home, Zeus helped Carly draw a bath in the master bathroom and then took a quick shower and started on dinner. He made something simple, something that would sit well after a tough day of stress.

When she came out of his bedroom, hair still damp and eyes glowing and refreshed, her curvy body clad in soft, comfortable sweats, she took his breath away.

He could imagine seeing her like this every morning. Waking up to her next to him in bed. He couldn't picture it any other way.

And the walks in the woods. The children or cubs

that could eventually come.

He was grateful for his military training and his bear, two different ways to protect the things that meant the most in his life.

He pulled out a chair for her and guided her into it. He served her, and as they ate, there was a comfortable friendliness between them that just kept affirming they'd made the right decision.

But there was also a tension slowly building, anticipation of more of the delicious pleasure they'd had between them the day before.

It seemed he couldn't keep his hands off her. Luckily, by the shy, sultry looks she was giving him from under her eyelashes, she seemed to feel the same way.

When they'd eaten most of the food, and it was growing dark and silent outside in the woods, he could feel the tension like electricity moving around them, dancing over his skin.

"How are you feeling?" Zeus asked Carly.

"Great," she said with a shy smile, the pressure in the room increasing every second Zeus saw her watching him. His soft, beautiful mate was perfect in every way.

And now he was going to claim her forever as his own.

Zeus stood and came over to where Carly was seated, then swooped her up into his arms, loving the feel of her soft curves against his skin, the light brush of her hair along his neck as she nestled into his arms.

"Shall we take this to the bedroom, then?" he asked.

Carly didn't say a word, just wrapped her hand around his neck and leaned forward, placing a kiss on his jaw. It made him smile, and as he walked toward their room, he could scent the slowly building arousal in the air. Her arousal.

Zeus intended to show her just how aroused she made him too.

He closed the door behind him and turned the lights to a gentle dimness that gave the room a subtle warmth. He wanted to see his mate when he took her.

To be one with his mate, finally. That was the only thought on his mind. That and pleasuring her every day for the rest of her life, as much as she could possibly receive, in every way imaginable. That was his mission.

He set Carly gently down on the bed and came over her, loving the sight of her beneath him, protected and surrounded by his arms. He could see fire in her eyes as he took off his shirt and removed her shirt and sweatpants immediately, leaving her only her in her underwear. Her skin was so soft, so wonderful, like velvet under his hands as he ran them over her body, drawing silent, sensuous sighs from her lips.

His bear was so close to the surface, roaring in approval. He would take her, soon. But first he wanted to pleasure her fully.

He undid the small clasp of Carly's bra and pulled it off. Her breasts were perfect to him, and holding them, touching them, squeezing them was ecstasy. Each lick over her nipples made him harder than iron; each kiss over their tortured tips made her moan and say his name into the silence of the night, his own personal fantasy.

Her scent surrounded them in the room. The scent of his Carly, his mate. Flowery and sweet but also special and unique. Like her.

He squeezed both breasts together, pressing his thumb over the nipples, and came over her on the bed to kiss her long and hard. She let out a gasp that was stifled by the kiss, and as he pressed into her lips, she moaned and arched against the bed in pleasure. Just the feel of her lips against his, the gentle pressure she exerted against him as he held her and ran his thumbs along her nipples and moved his tongue inside her mouth, was perfection.

Zeus left her mouth and kissed the small spot at the base of her ear that made her body jerk with arousal. He still held her breasts in his hands, not wanting to let them go, the feel of them so tantalizing and irresistible.

Irresistible. Everything about his mate was irresistible.

By now, Carly's breath had quickened substantially, and every touch, every kiss made her gasp. He sat up and looked down at her, enjoying the feel of her curvy hips between his thighs.

His mate was so small, so special. He'd always protect her, always keep her safe. Always love everything about her and do everything in his power to make her happy.

"Zeus, this is so amazing. But you still owe me from the other night," Carly said playfully, eyeing the bulge in his pants with lust.

He knew the second he entered her, his bear would be in full control, ravenous and insatiable until they'd both come together and were sealed as one. He wanted to hold off a little longer, make sure she was ready. But at the same time, every second he saw her like this beneath his hands brought him closer to losing control.

Zeus brought his hand between her legs and ran it under her panties, holding her center and flicking one finger over her clit, making her hips buck futilely against him. Her hands flailed as he did, and he took both her wrists in his free hand and pinned them above her, holding them in place. She smiled up at him in approval.

He ran his finger once more against her, and she moaned ever more loudly, the intensity increased from being held in place by his long, powerful arms.

"Tell me you're mine forever," Zeus commanded as he held his finger right over her clit and held it there. He knew Carly would never run out on him, never abandon him. But he wanted to hear it from her lips. Wanted to hear her say she was just as much his as he was hers and would be for all time.

"I'm yours forever, Zeus," she said hoarsely. The sight of her almost-naked body, writhing in ecstasy and completely overcome by the pleasure he gave her, was euphoric.

He ran his index finger against her clit once more, a long, smooth stroke, and she came apart in his arms, orgasming with incredible strength. He let her arms go, and she wrapped herself around him, holding him tightly.

"Zeus, oh, Zeus," she cried out, enraptured.

As she came, he held her close, admiring and enjoying the feel of her body. She screamed and clawed at his back, but this pain, unlike any other Zeus had experienced before in his life, was pleasurable. The feel of her nails as they dug in was evidence of the all-encompassing pleasure that he alone gave her.

Her body finally relaxed, and he dipped his hand below her waist again. He could feel her wetness, knew just how ready she was for him, turning him on even more, past the point of being able to wait any longer. His bear roared inside.

It was time to claim his mate.

* * *

Zeus was everywhere. And the faster he went, the more he did, the more Carly wanted—no, needed— him inside. Needed him to quench the fire that had been building in her all night, even since the last time they were together. To feel his hard, thick length inside her, stroking her and filling her.

The previous orgasm had been so strong and overwhelming that she had lost control and probably scratched him pretty deeply. But Zeus didn't seem to have any complaints, and as he looked down at her, it was like she could see eternity in his eyes, those blue depths going on and on, watching her with love that was never ending.

Zeus came off the bed and undid his pants. Already, she'd been admiring the breadth of his shoulders, the definition of his muscles in his upper body, and it left her wanting to see the lower half again. She was almost giddy with excitement.

As he lowered the zipper, his member sprang free, reminding her just how well-endowed he was. How had she been able to fit that inside last time?

He took off his pants and crawled onto the bed, kneeling before her, his perfect body on full display, making her even more wet than she already was.

"After this, it's you and me, Carly. Always," Zeus said, his voice husky and deep as he watched her, devouring her with his eyes.

"Always." Carly loved the sound of it. The knowledge that this incredible, overwhelming man would always be hers and hers alone was mind-blowing.

Almost as mind-blowing as the sex.

Zeus slid her panties off and came over her, giving her a perfect view of his pecs and arms as he propped himself above her. He teased at her entrance, and she could feel just how hard he was, could almost taste the perfect pleasure having him inside gave her.

With one smooth motion, he slid inside, all the way until their hips were joined together. Zeus was just the perfect size, and every ridge, every inch of him heated her up and filled her with an intense, burning sensation across her entire body.

This was even better than she remembered.

For a moment, Zeus paused, letting Carly adjust to his size. Then he began a slow, intense rhythm that blew her mind completely. Each time he came out, she felt her body beg for more, which he immediately answered by stroking back in, powerful and smooth, and letting her enjoy every sweet sensation his cock gave her. All of her nerves were alight with pleasure and delicious tension, so much more than she could fathom.

But she wanted more. She wanted faster. She wanted so badly to see Zeus come it was all she could think about.

As Zeus pushed down into her, she moved her hips up against him, doubling the speed of their friction. Zeus tensed and smiled at her. Then, with a low growl, he moved faster, his normal calm and control replaced with raw, animal lust. It was a side of him she'd only seen a few times. Only when protecting her or when they were together like this. His bear.

Carly looked forward to a lifetime of drawing out this part of him as much as she could in the bedroom. She relished the sight of him as he lost control, as his instincts took over and plundered her completely.

Faster and faster Zeus moved inside her, and she felt her body careening past its limits and so close, so close to coming. But she bit down on her lip and held on to to Zeus's ripped shoulders and focused on the sound of his breathing growing more and more rapid by the second. The slight sheen of sweat across his chiseled body. The possessive, carnal look in his eyes as he watched her, dominating her and owning her with every stroke.

Her entire body felt like a rubber band, stretched to its very limit with pleasure. She looked into Zeus's beautiful blue eyes, then saw him reach a finger down between them and flick up her center. She lost control, and her entire body was consumed with exquisite pleasure. A split second later, she felt Zeus jerk inside her as all his muscles tensed at the same time, filling her with warmth as his seed spilled into her.

Carly held on to Zeus's arms as wave after wave of release washed through her, by far the most powerful orgasm of her entire life. The two of them going together like this was beyond words, beyond definition. Even as the pleasure slowly subsided and left her feeling satisfied and euphoric and happy all over, the magic of it overwhelmed her.

Zeus stayed inside for a moment longer and came down, kissing her long and softly over her lips, as if sealing everything they'd just done together with an act of wonderful finality. The promise of forever.

Zeus slowly came out and moved to turn off the lights.

"Damn, if that's your bear, you need to let him out more often," Carly said as she relaxed into the plush, comfortable bed while Zeus came next to her and pulled the sheets over them.

Zeus chuckled in response. "Well, that's certainly possible. Tomorrow we'll complete the final ceremony in private in the woods, and it will be just you and me after that," he said contentedly.

"Just the two of us." Carly couldn't stop saying it. Like she had to keep reminding herself and validating the truth of the matter. Zeus was hers. What an inconceivable concept.

From the moment he'd first walked into the bar,

she'd never guessed this could happen. Which just made it all the more wonderful.

Zeus wrapped an arm around her and curled her next to him. She felt so warm and safe there. Perhaps every day was going to feel this unreal, being with such a wonderful, protective, caring man. But if it was, she was glad Zeus was always going to be there by her side, reminding her it really wasn't all a dream. Glad that he would be there to pinch her to make sure she wasn't going to wake up.

"I love you, Carly," he whispered to her as she nestled closer to him. "With all my heart."

"I love you too, Zeus," she whispered in the cool darkness as night settled over the room and the forest around them. Outside, the moon peeked through the drapes, hovering over the forest surrounding them.

So long as the sun rose and the moon shone, she would be Zeus's. And he would be hers. Her big, bad bear. Her good-hearted soldier.

Her love.

* * *

* * *

Hi, thanks so much for reading Zeus and Carly's story. I hope you enjoyed it and if you did I hope you'll leave a review for it to help others find it! It really helps me as an author.

Ares's story will be out soon, so make sure you're signed up with my newsletter here:

http://eepurl.com/3KYtH

Thanks again for your support!

Sincerely,

Terry Bolryder

Terry's Facebook

ABOUT THE AUTHOR

Terry Bolryder loves reading and writing fun paranormal romances with big-hearted heroes, and has the best readers in the world. Thanks for your support!

12151202R00104

Printed in Great Britain
by Amazon.co.uk, Ltd.,
Marston Gate.